Sophie Hardy and the Internet Implant

M.R. Dale

www.sophiehardysaga.com

For Clara

Prologue – 10 Years Ago – The Departure

Jane was holding the baby she was to become godmother to. They were in the hospital and Clara was barely eight hours old, but Jane knew that what she was about to do would turn the small child's life upside down in so many ways that she didn't know where to start counting.

She looked at the new-born bundle of joy in her arms and wished she could think of another way to do what she was about to do. Clara's eyes were closed, and she gently wriggled her nose and curled her lip as she lay sleeping peacefully. Just outside the door, Clara's parents had stepped out to fulfil their work obligations at a time of such heightened tension and nervousness; Earth would be thrown into complete carnage and chaos if Jane and Clara's parents didn't carry out their respective mission.

Second thoughts littered her head once more. She couldn't do it. Doing what her bosses had told her would mean that Clara's parents were sure to disappear and never see her again, for they would be cast out to a place unbeknown even to Jane. Her boss had promised her that what she was about to do was out of necessity, not just for the agency but for the safety of the planet itself.

'The agents will be uploaded to Stratus,' he had said, 'Their physical forms will vanish, but they will still be alive...ish but not around to put everything on Earth in mortal danger.'

Changing her grip on the baby, Jane took out a small white ball with what appeared to be green and red liquid flowing around inside it from her pocket and rolled it around her hand. This was the only possible way she could think of to give Clara even an outside chance to be with her parents once she flicked the switch that would bring about their departure, but she didn't even know if that was going to work! She could be about to subject this newly born infant to either a life with no biological parents or no life at all! Her choice was impossible. She closed her eyes and contemplated some more.

The world was about to be overrun. Even her husband had messaged her to tell her that the most feared creature in all the universe was arriving and judgement was about to be served to humanity and the way they had chosen to live – in conflict with those that weren't the same as them. 'The agents, the mythicals and the planet must be sealed off to save us all,' her boss had told her.

The mythicals were bad. Jane had been told that much by everyone she had ever met, and she had carried out every mission she had ever been given with never a question asked or grievance muttered despite the suffering it brought to mythicals the world over. Surely this was too much though? Taking two parents away from their child? Sealing Earth off from everyone? Banishing mythical creatures to a life of pain and anguish? All of it was designed to keep out one threat because none of the agents could be trusted any longer or so her boss had said to have them removed as well.

Earlier that evening, Jane had rounded up one more mythical and separated yet another family but that was for their own good... so she was told. The mythical was a danger just like all the others. Clara's parents weren't, they were just in the way, in the wrong place at the wrong time and had the wrong opinion on important matters and so would have to suffer the consequences. They thought differently than her boss and that was enough for him to want them gone.

'Nobody harms my company, my agency,' he would say.

If, though, this plan Jane had concocted ad hock worked, the family would be at least together albeit in the most unusual way.

The rolling of the spherical invention in Jane's hand got faster as the thoughts gathered momentum. Taking Clara over to the window to show her the world, it didn't appear to be on the brink of disaster, but Jane knew better. It was one little girl spending her life with her parents versus the safety of civilisation itself. It was a no-brainer. She stuck the small white ball to the side of Clara's head and sat down with her in the chair next to the bed her mum had been resting in and watched the sun begin to set.

Jane shut her eyes and activated "the hub of the internet" she had attached to Clara's head. All she had to do now was click the green button on the long, screwdriver-like device, which she took out of her pocket and held in her other hand and all the agents, and hopefully, Clara, would be locked away until a time when Earth was safe, and she or her boss would be able to set them free. She stroked Clara's head and kissed her tiny hand. Then another dark thought hit. The agents would be safe, but they would be so angry with her. She was about to take them away, destroying their lives for the sake of a different viewpoint. Jane instantly began to question how she could possibly face them ever again. Until they were freed, they would be able to contact her but she would be unable to do anything about it as she would have no idea where they were. The messages would be horrendous – angry, desperate pleas to be freed but Jane wouldn't know how. She was locking them away but didn't have the key, or even any idea of where the door was. It was then she vowed to turn off the messages. They would be unbearable to read through and the guilt and burden they would place on her would be insurmountable.

Making the promise to herself to never read them, she focused once more on Clara, 'I promise to look after you if this doesn't work,' she whispered softly, 'Everything is up to me now. I just hope I don't let you down.'

Without another second's thought, she activated the hub on Clara's head, and it glowed a bright white. Clara was completely undisturbed by it all. Jane knew that sending her away like this wouldn't hurt her and so she smiled.

'Go,' she whispered as she pressed the green button.

Immediately, the lights in the room flashed and the bulbs smashed into a thousand pieces. The windows rattled as did the furniture in the room. Jane leant over Clara to protect her from the shards of glass that fell from the ceiling. Clara opened her eyes and for a split-second, they were bright white. Jane caught sight of them and wondered what on Earth had happened. Almost instantly, Clara's eyes returned to their gorgeous blue and she closed them again and carried on sleeping.

Whatever Jane was expecting to happen hadn't. Either Clara was supposed to disappear before her eyes and be with her parents or nothing was supposed to happen. She hadn't anticipated flashing lights and eyes. Something wasn't right.

To check that what she had done had actually worked, Jane stood up with Clara still in her arms and walked towards the door. Opening it, she looked out to see whether Clara's mum and dad were still out in the corridor. They were. They were wondering what the earthquake-like tremor had been. Jane caught their eye and reassured them that everything was fine with Clara and that they were to complete their task. The agent's and Clara's upload to Stratus hadn't worked. Whatever pressing the green button had done to Clara, it hadn't done what it was supposed to have done to everyone else. The bodies of the agents were meant to vanish, and the consciences be uploaded but Clara's parents were still out there.

She carried Clara back into the room and sat back down on the chair. Immediately, Jane zoned out on her modified mark I implant by staring at that empty space people can see between them and the objects in front of them and pressed the *virtual* go button this time, before taking a deep breath to see if it had worked at the second time of asking.

Zoning back into the room, she noticed Clara was still in her arms and sleeping happily just like she had been. She made for the door again and opened it quietly so as not to draw attention to herself. Straight away she noticed that there was nobody standing where Clara's mum and dad had been before. The device had worked on them, but Clara was still with her. Jane immediately resigned herself to the idea of Clara being without a mum and dad and took out the hub of the internet that she had placed on the side of her head. Then, she placed it in her pocket and knew that it would need to be in place in Stratus in minutes.

She messaged her boss to tell him that the job was complete. There wasn't an instantaneous reply; eventually, a simple message came through that read, 'Thank you'.

Jane walked over with Clara to the window and looked at the sunset again. It had turned an unusual shade of blue and screams, yelps and cries could now be heard across the city. Sounds that Jane knew she had brought about to keep Earth safe.

'What have I done?' she asked herself and Clara.

Across the road, a family of four elves were writhing around on the floor covering their ears in agony. Before Jane could look any closer, the elves simply disappeared before her eyes.

Confused, as that also wasn't what she was expecting to happen, Jane turned back to Clara and a new worry set in. She had no idea what to do with her. She had basically orphaned this little girl and didn't know what to do.

She only had one option – take her to her old friends from school who had just got married – Matthew and Joshua. They would know what to do with her. They had no other children, but Jane knew that Matthew's sister, Amelia, had just been told that she was expecting a baby soon and so Clara would at least have a sibling of sorts.

Silently, Jane opened the black door, which had a diamond window, into the corridor and took Clara to go and lead a completely new, unexpected life. As she did so, Clara's eyes opened and again glowed white for a second. If Jane didn't know better, she would have said she smiled at her. With no idea what had happened to Clara the first time she had pressed the green button, Jane knew now that she owed her a great debt and the best way to repay it would be to give her a good home and a chance in the future to maybe, maybe, see her parents again... wherever it was that Jane had sent them.

Chapter 1 – Present Day – 10 Years After The Departure – The Beginning of the Beginning

Her fists clenched and her face reddened, Sophie Hardy was livid at the situation that life had put her in. Having just turned 10 last week, she was demanding to know from her bemused dad, Tom, why she wasn't allowed the latest, must-have gadget whereas her mum, Amelia, was allowed to sit there and waste away on it. Twenty minutes the argument had been going; words had been thrown and demands issued.

'But we don't make the rules, Soph,' Tom replied, in an effort to soothe the situation, 'no child in the world is allowed one until they're eleven!'

'But just look at her!' Sophie screeched aiming her finger at her mum. 'She doesn't do anything! She just sits there completely oblivious to all of us! The least she could do is something useful if she's going to have that much knowledge available to her and spend her life ignoring us! I could do all sorts with one of those!'

'I know, dear,' said Tom, struggling to argue back as he knew his daughter was right.

'You know I don't argue much...' Sophie began to reason with her dad, but Tom looked at her through his eyebrows. 'Well...

not that much! But I *am* right about this! It's the last day of the six-week holiday and she has done nothing with us all day!'

Sophie knew that this wasn't what life was supposed to be about and what made this even more frustrating for her was that she was right; the Internet Implant would make *her* life more exciting and give her immediate access to any piece of information she desired, and this thought made Sophie's heart dance. Tom knew it would help his daughter as well, but she wasn't allowed one; this though wasn't any fault of his.

The implant had been released nine years ago to anyone over the age of 11 by Shadow (the world's largest tech company), which was headed by the self-proclaimed 'Smartest Man on the Planet', Alton King and his lesser known, but just as clever, assistant – Dale Natan. It was a tiny piece of technology that was installed in a person's head and allowed them access to the internet 24/7 from inside their own mind. The basic version brought a new, fully interactive, 3D experience to even mundane tasks like typing something in on a search engine.

No phones, laptops or tablets were needed anymore – unless you were under 11 years old. People just started surfing the internet from inside their own imaginations and everything popped up, quite literally, in front of their eyes.

'Dad, she doesn't do anything on it!' Sophie appealed, 'she's just been sitting there all day! She'll just be watching videos or finding arguments that nobody should really have!' Sophie's contentions were starting to repeat themselves.

However, Tom looked at Amelia in the chair and again found it difficult to argue with Sophie's point.

'All that knowledge out there!' Sophie started again, 'I could use that! But Mum is just wasting away doing nothing!'

'You get one when you're 11,' Tom calmly reasoned back, 'And who knows what tomorrow might bring!' he said with a twinkle in his eye that Sophie would have spotted had she not been so cross.

'Why doesn't Mum want to spend time with me and Lizzie?' Sophie said with sad eyes looking over at her baby sister who was sitting in her swing in the door frame with her bottom lip wobbling, about to burst into tears – she hated it when people shouted.

The sight of Lizzie brought about a few seconds of sombre silence and Sophie was then more frustrated than angry. She knew it wasn't her dad's fault, but she had to take this annoyance out on someone, and he just happened to be in the wrong place at the wrong time!

'I want to learn about the mythicals,' Sophie said, much more serenely than her arguments previously and Tom nodded in understanding.

Her fascination with knowledge, living life to the full and wanting to better herself stemmed from the stories Tom had been telling her since she was tiny. They were all about how, not many years ago, there were monsters (Dad and the rest of the adult population had referred to them as 'mythicals') that had roamed the planet, some causing panic and disruption, others flat-out on wanting to take over the world, but then, one day, they all just vanished and nobody it seemed knew why or even seemed to care anymore.

'I want to know why people don't talk about them anymore. I want to know why centaurs, goblins, aliens and ghosts don't dominate people's minds like they used to!' Sophie explained and Tom could see that he had more than sparked her curiosity over the years, 'Why is it only you who does it, Dad?'

'I don't know, Soph,' Tom said, still siding with Sophie and not wanting to extinguish this fiery curiosity that he could see raging through his daughter.

'I don't want to waste away like Mum is,' Sophie concluded.

Pushing her blonde hair off her face, Sophie relaxed slightly as the nonsensical fury that had taken over her began to fade away. Her green eyes were gradually returning from the red they had become, and her body was a lot less stiff. Calm had just about returned to the Hardy residence.

After what had felt like hours, but was actually nanoseconds, Sophie decided to leave the room and stand on the balcony of their twelfth-floor flat on the old part of the Pinkleton estate, to allow herself to completely relax. As she shuffled over to the sliding doors, Tom knew where she was going – it was where Sophie always went when she wanted to escape the slightly harsh reality that had become her life. She didn't want a lot, which was a good job as her family couldn't afford much! She just knew that she could do so much if life would just give her opportunity to. Even if *that* opportunity wasn't presented, then she lived in hope that her mum would want to actually spend time with her!

On top of this, year 6 tests were coming up this year, so Sophie needed a break – something amazing needed to happen. Although she loved her teacher, throughout Year 5 she was constantly telling her that she needed to focus and do well on the tests or the world might actually end! This was even though Sophie strived for self-improvement so much that she was towards the top of the class. So, because of her desire to stay there and do well in her assessments, she was going to find school stressful when she started back tomorrow.

A gentle breeze brushed against Sophie's face and another worry reared its ugly head in her mind. Money in the house was also causing unnecessary stress for a girl of her age. Her dad didn't earn much from his job in a factory – Sophie wasn't exactly sure what he did, and he often complained about how boring it was but, 'a job's a job,' he always said. Her mum always talked about getting a job when she wasn't zoned out, but nothing ever really materialised, most likely because Amelia was very busy looking after Sophie and her baby sister (who still loved waking up in the middle of the night for a snack on a bottle, therefore, making Amelia tired!) or, more likely, surfing on the internet. So, her parents' job situation meant that Sophie didn't have too many luxuries in her life, but she did have a family and for that, she was very grateful.

With all these things going on in Sophie's life, it would be tough for an adult to stay sane at the minute, never mind a 10-year-old!

After giving Sophie a few minutes on her own to calm herself, Tom stepped out onto the balcony as well.

'I just want to be better, Dad,' Sophie said as Tom slid the door closed behind him. He then said nothing, he just leaned on the balcony looking over the village.

Taking in the air that she got from being that high up on a calm evening and looking into the horizon, she saw the final blue flickers of sunlight for the day. The blues seemed to be dancing from one colour to another.

'You know,' Tom said, trying to change the subject, 'the sky never used to be this shade of blue and it never danced like this!'

Sophie nodded; her dad had told her this story plenty of times before.

'It just changed one night about ten years ago,' Tom continued to explain, 'no experts or anyone could explain it and since the implant nobody has really tried to.'

Sophie couldn't help but see that humanity now seemed that engrossed in their online worlds that they just seemed to accept things like the sky changing colour – it wasn't doing them any harm so why would they need to worry about it or change it?

Seeing that he wasn't getting any sort of response from Sophie, Tom reasoned that she needed some more time by herself and so went back inside to see to Lizzie.

Sophie then realised just how ungrateful she had been to her dad. He always put her first and always did everything he could for her. *It isn't worth it*, Sophie thought to herself. *No one my age has one, it's not like I'm missing out. And anyway, I'll be getting one in less than twelve months now, and then I can start challenging myself, not like everyone else.*

Sheepishly, she turned to go back indoors and offer an apology to Tom. Sophie was extremely grown up for her age and had no trouble being the first to apologise. Sliding back the huge glass door, she ran straight into Tom's arms and gave him a cuddle. No words were exchanged - they just hugged it out.

After a while, Tom kissed Sophie's head and said with genuine enthusiasm, 'School tomorrow.'

It was Monday today, but the teachers were having a training day, so school was to start on Tuesday.

'I saw Yasmine's parents and Katie's mum the other day. Apparently, Mr Houghton has got some sort of surprise task for the first day, some visitor from somewhere,' Tom said like he knew what it was and wanted to tell Sophie but wasn't going to say.

A rather unenthusiastic, year 6 'ooh' was Sophie's reply, 'Haven't we heard from Uncle Matthew and Uncle Josh yet?' she asked.

Now that the conversation had shifted back to school, Sophie decided to ask again about her uncles and her cousin.

At the start of the six-week holiday, Sophie's cousin – Clara Betts - who Sophie had been extremely close to, had just moved house with her two dads to the other side of the city for some reason unbeknown to Sophie and she missed them all hugely. The two were the same age and had spent all their primary school lives together in the same class every year, in the same groups for everything and were practically inseparable in school and out. It was most unlike Clara and her dads to just up sticks and leave without any notice. Someone had simply pushed a note under the door of the Hardy flat about five weeks ago saying they were moving to 'get a change' - whatever that meant!

'No,' Tom replied, 'Mum's tried to ring them but there's no answer and she said that she went around there last week, and the house looked immaculate but unlived in!'

Sophie shook her head, annoyed that Clara didn't even say 'goodbye', but something in the back of her mind told her that all wasn't as it seemed.

Whilst Sophie and Tom were talking about Clara, Matthew and Joshua, Amelia eventually zoned back into the room and looked at her husband and eldest daughter and saw straight away there had been some upset in the flat.

'Come on, I'll tell you another story from 'the olden days', Tom said, trying to avoid a confrontation between his wife and daughter.

Sophie's eyes lit up.

'Aliens or gods tonight? What about another tale of the child-snatchers who got banished to the underworld for the horrendous acts they committed on countless innocent children and how they have been prophesied to return when the mythicals find the power to do so?' Tom asked with delight dancing in his eyes.

'Mythicals!' Sophie replied with a lot more enthusiasm.

'OK...' Tom began, baffled as that hadn't exactly been one of the choices, but the two went off to her room for her bedtime story nonetheless.

'They say that Echidna was a creature with the body of a human but no legs, only a tail like a snake. The humans were so scared of her and the power she commanded over the mythicals that they gave her the title The Mother of Monsters...' Tom continued.

Sophie listened intently to every word as she lay in her bed while her dad spoke with such great enthusiasm. She absorbed the knowledge and the story like always. Filing it in her memory, she would replay it over and over. If only she could be offered one chance, just one, to better herself or to spend time with her mum.

The disappearance of the mythicals still didn't make sense to her no matter how much she thought about it, and neither did the fact that her mum didn't seem to want her. So once again, with all her other worries still prominent, she fell asleep questioning everything about the planet around her.

Chapter 2 – First Day Back

As a treat for her starting year 6, Sophie's mum and dad had agreed that she could start walking to school without them if she agreed to go with two of her friends whose parents had made the same decision. It would have been three friends had Clara still been around but that wasn't to be. So, as the lift reached the ground floor of Sophie's block of flats and the door slid open, there, waiting for Sophie, were Yasmine Ariti and Katie Brown.

Yasmine was very loud and came across as extremely confident but underneath her strong-minded persona, she was very shy and was even sometimes unsure of herself. Although she hid this very well from those that didn't know her. People sometimes thought that Yasmine could be a bit bossy and loud, but this couldn't be further from the truth. She was an extremely caring person who just let her confidence come out when she wasn't concentrating, but when she realised, she reigned it back in again. Yasmine's family were a lot richer than Sophie's. Her dad, Nicholas, whose mum (Yasmine's grandmother) had come over from Greece when her dad was little, was always out of the country 'on business' but the girls didn't really know exactly what he did. Yasmine's best guess was that he worked for some major company in some capacity getting famous people to advertise the latest upgrade or patch for the Internet Implant but beyond that, she wasn't sure. He had mentioned mythical creatures very briefly in passing before but never as much as Sophie's dad did. Yasmine's long, flowing dark brown almost black hair and light brown complexion reminded her of her Mediterranean roots, which her dad took very seriously.

Katie on the other hand was very, very shy. She only really spoke out loud in front of Sophie and Yasmine (or Clara when she was around) and even then, her comments were brief. When it came to the classroom, Katie kept herself to herself and didn't want to put her hand up. She was clever but, unfortunately for her, her three friends were *really* clever and it made it look like she wasn't gifted. As a result, Katie always wore her long, fiery red hair down to try and hide her face, in an effort to make her teachers not notice her.

When she was younger, Katie's dad had left and neither she nor her mum had seen him since. She had heard he was living in the town up the road and that he had a new girlfriend, but he had made little effort to contact her and showed no evidence of wanting to see her other than a birthday card each year, which always came a few days late. This lack of a father had hit Katie's self-confidence hard, which explained her quietness; she was though, a lot better than she had been. Looking after her mum, Tasha, and mum looking after her, the pair of them had formed a rock-solid bond living on their own for all that time. As Katie was getting older and was now about to become one of the oldest at school, Sophie wished that she would start showing even more improvement in her confidence and self-belief and spend less time worrying about how worthless she thought she was and how she had spent so long thinking that nobody wanted her.

Dressed in their unique, lilac-coloured school jumpers and black trousers, Katie and Yasmine turned and followed Sophie out of the building with only a muttered '*Hey*' between the three of them.

It was the first day back and none of them were particularly looking forward to it. Another whole year of 'You need to pass this maths test or it'll look bad on you,' or 'You need to pass this grammar test or you won't be able to write properly.' Sophie could tell from her teacher's voice that she didn't actually believe what she was saying and in a weird way she respected her for it. However, no child was excited at the prospect of year 6 - the year of tests and the last year of glorious primary school.

As they walked in near silence, no one noticed anymore the damage which had been done to the local church about twenty years ago – it was all just something that existed in the background now. The adults had briefly told the very hazy story about how a giant had gotten loose and trodden on it before being chased away by the angry villagers. Sophie had heard many different stories about the olden days but this one she found particularly hard to believe. She thought it was just people in Pinkleton trying to make life sound more exciting. It just sounded less believable than some of her dad's other stories such as: 'The Draining of Venice - 1970' or 'Code Blackpool – Terror on the Tower'.

Neither Katie nor Yasmine were as intrigued by the history of the planet as Sophie was. Despite Yasmine's dad heralding from Greece – the place most synonymous with mythical creatures on Earth – he just didn't seem to remember what it used to be like when the mythicals were around so Yasmine never really bothered asking. Sophie was sure she would be intrigued if she just decided to listen and pay attention but Yasmine never acted on it despite Sophie's appeals. Katie, on the other hand, was much too busy supporting her mum, who was working at least two jobs, to be interested in anything much else. Both of the two girls were very well aware of Sophie's desire to find out more and for them, it bordered on obsession.

With it being the first-time they had walked to school together, the three of them didn't really notice the huge increase in the amount of traffic that was on the road that morning. Lots of self-driving cars (another Shadow invention that had crept in over the last ten years) and vans were making their way through the village of Pinkleton in the same direction as the three girls but Sophie, Yasmine and Katie all remained oblivious. Sophie just kept catching sight of people on buses or in cars zoned out using their implants when they could have been looking at the world around them. After her outburst last night, Sophie kept a lid on her grievance and carried on walking as another lorry drove past and turned up the road towards school. She did try to tell the story of 'The Mother of Monsters' to the other two but they weren't particularly bothered so Sophie stayed quiet.

When they rounded the corner that lead to the school field, the conversation suddenly sprang into life about what greeted them. Peering as best they could through the thick hedge and tall green fence that separated the school field from the road, the girls could see that there were countless trucks and trailers with what looked like film crews carrying cameras and sound mics running around attempting to get organised for something. There was a hum of busyness about the school as hundreds, maybe thousands, of people were shouting instructions to each other from one end of the field to the other.

'What's all this?' Katie chirped in.

'My mum said that there was something going off today but she couldn't or wouldn't tell me what,' Yasmine replied.

'Yeah, she told my dad about it. In fact, he said your mum was there as well Katie,' said Sophie inquisitively.

Katie just shrugged as she genuinely had no idea what Sophie was talking about.

Sophie pondered about what or indeed who would be so important as to bring all this attention to the school field in the unremarkable village of Pinkleton.

Pinkleton was a medium-sized village in the middle of England. Not a lot happened there; occasionally there was a village fayre. Around July time each year, there was the village music festival – 'Pinklefest' – which consisted of local musicians trying to recreate the hits of their favourite bands. Most of the time it was a group of pensioners all singing completely out of tune or students from Pinkleton High School singing an indecipherable racket but really, everybody loved it. There was the odd time it got on the local news for something completely uneventful but, on the whole, nothing happened in Pinkleton. Along with the rest of the world nowadays, it was all quite boring compared to what life sounded like around the time the girls were born. So, all this business on the school field was most intriguing to the local residents who were slowly starting to form a crowd behind the tall fence that encased the hedge around the field. It seemed like the entire village had turned up and were desperately squinting through trying to get a better look.

Most intrigued were the three girls. They picked up the pace, walked quickly round to the main gate, almost ran up the drive, which was on a steep slope, and arrived on the school playground. It was on the opposite side of the school to the field but still out of sight of the road due to its elevated position. They were just about to join the rest of school and make a dash for the path that led to the back of the school to peer through at the hive of activity on the field, before Mrs Tabard, the school's dinner lady, bell ringer, office manager, part-time caretaker and even, on special occasions, DJ, rang the bell to signal that it was time to line up.

Annoyed at the fact that they had missed out on a good stare, Sophie, Yasmine and Katie found their new line for the year and helped a few Foundation Stage children find their line (as was expected of the year sixes). Surrounded by emotional Foundation Stage parents wishing their four-year-olds all the best as if they were sending them off into war, the girls asked other pupils what the drama was on the school field. Nobody knew, or at least that's what they made out, but the crowds grew larger still. Sophie leant over to Ryan Myers, the boy in year 6 that nobody really wanted to sit next to because his behaviour was so bad, and tried to ask him if he knew anything, but before she could get the question out, Mrs Tabard bellowed at her for even thinking about talking.

It had long been Mrs Tabard's dream to be a teacher but many people assumed that she thought she was passed it, didn't have the qualifications and so did any other job around school she could while dreaming of being a class teacher.

A few seconds later, the silence descended from eerie to numbing as the teachers emerged from the school, which was up a slope from the playground the children were all lined up on. The children gazed up at them and some of the Foundation Stage even started crying (along with their parents) as the teachers came down to meet the children. Arriving in front of each class, the teachers stood as smart as they could, trying to set a good example. Mrs Tabard was still monitoring the noise level and kept barking at some of the younger children, who would now never dream of standing with their hands in their pockets again in their lives! Eventually, Mr Houghton, the head teacher, bounded out of the school with bundles of enthusiasm. He virtually skipped down the steps, which was quite unusual to watch as he wasn't a small man; in fact, he was enormous. He towered over the children by about three clear feet and had arms like tree trunks. His slick brown hair was parted immaculately at the side and his boyish charm infected the playground.

'Take them in everyone, take these wonderful children in. Get them educated!' he beamed as he went over and introduced himself to some of the parents of the little ones that were still crying as their children skipped happily inside for their first day.

All the teachers, except one, rolled their eyes at the over-exuberance from the head, tutted and asked their class to follow them. The one teacher that didn't react grumpily like that was Sophie's teacher – Miss Sissins – she simply smiled at the children reassuringly and winked at them. Sophie and the girls had been taught by her in year 5 and she had kindly volunteered to follow them into year 6 and help them do the best they could in order to make year 6 as bearable as possible. She was the one that made learning fun for the children. They knew absolutely nothing about her life outside of school and none of them had ever bumped into her or knew if she had a wife or husband but they all enjoyed her class. She was the shoulder to cry on if someone had upset you or the one to boost your confidence if you were feeling down on yourself. Even Katie had come slightly out of her shell with her last year. Her hair was dark and curly but short and going grey at the temples. She was only short; her skin was the darkest Sophie had ever seen and her eyes varied between friendly and approachable to teacher stare in a heartbeat depending on whether she had her glasses on or not. She pointed with her head towards the school, telling the class to follow; she then turned on her heel and led them inside.

Itching to ask Miss Sissins what on earth was going on, the class all scampered in and found their seats. Being in the same room as last year, the class just automatically drifted into last year's chairs and awaited eagerly the news they hoped Miss Sissins would bring.

Chapter 3 – The News

Miss Sissins did the register and then sent Ryan Myers down to the office to take it, it was custom for him to take the register in order to give him a job to do. Mrs Tabard appeared at the door a few minutes later demanding dinner money and letters from anyone that was on 'the list' – including Ryan despite him just having taken the register down! Everyone paid up instantly but they were all a bit baffled at the idea that they might have letters to return and dinner money debts to pay on the first day back.

After the kerfuffle with Mrs Tabard, Miss Sissins turned to face a class of children that were perched on the edge of their seats almost drooling with anticipation of what was happening on the field.

'I take it you've all seen the field?' Miss Sissins asked, knowing full well they all had.

'Yes' came the response from the class (except for Ryan who just shrugged and pretended he wasn't bothered). They all shuffled even further forward on their chairs - they were practically hovering in front of them.

'Well, you know how Mr Houghton can get excited about things that aren't that exciting and tends to waffle on about things for forty minutes but could have been done in five?'

The whole school, practically the whole village, knew that Mr Houghton liked to talk; however, the children thought he was wonderful and his chatting had become a bit of a running joke, especially amongst the older children. Although as Miss Sissins said this, they slumped in their chairs as they could feel a huge anti-climax coming.

'This *isn't* one of those occasions,' Miss Sissins said.

The whole class sat bolt upright again and Miss Sissins carried on, 'Here, in our humble village, are some people from Shadow... well... one person,' she said enthusiastically, waving her hands about as she talked like she always did when talking about something she thought was exciting 'on our very own playground, is the man himself, the inventor of the Internet Implant – Alton King.'

The class fell about themselves. They accused Miss Sissins of lying, and thought she was joking and pulling their legs, but she assured them she wasn't.

Miss Sissins continued her enlightenment, 'Shadow, well Mr King, said they wanted a village primary school somewhere in England to announce some news about the company and so ran a competition for schools to enter and apply. Mr Houghton entered our school and we were chosen!'

Exhilaration grew exponentially within the class. The children would be the envy of anyone and everyone they knew at other schools and could live off this for years. The world's media and Alton King – the richest, smartest man on Earth - were on *their* field.

'When do we get to go outside and see?' Yasmine asked brushing her hair with her fingers in an effort to make it smart for the cameras.

Miss Sissins looked at the clock and began counting on her fingers; she must have reached about fifteen before putting her fingers down and quite calmly said, 'Oh, in about two minutes.'

Never had so many girls, and indeed boys asked to go to the toilet and do their hair so quickly. There was a mad rush for every mirror. Five minutes later, all the children were back in their seats looking a lot less like it was the first time they had gotten up early in six weeks than they did a few minutes before. There was only Katie who hadn't made a move for a mirror.

'Are you ready to go outside now?' asked Miss Sissins.

'Err, yes,' Sophie and Yasmine said in perfect unison as if affectionately talking to an idiot.

Miss Sissins smiled as she knew the two of them so well to know they were just excited and said 'OK then, straight line at the door.'

Yasmine and Sophie leapt to the front.

'Yazz and Soph, you will have to go at the back.'

'What for?' Yasmine asked, nervously.

'Being cheeky by talking to me like that,' Miss Sissins replied with a smug look on her face.

The pair crumpled their mouths in fake anger and took themselves to the back as Miss Sissins mimicked their facial expressions. Everyone else smiled and rolled their eyes.

After a few squabbles and a bit of pushing, Class 6 was ready to go out and take part in history. The idea that Alton King was here was enough distraction for most of the children, however, Sophie had thought beyond that and was more thinking why? *Why would he want a school?* The children quietened down completely and started snaking out of the door onto the field, with Miss Sissins at the head of the line. Anticipation grew.

Being in the classroom that was the furthest away from the field, year 6 arrived at the field last out of all the classes and they saw all the other children from school spread out on the grass all staring up at something. They were used to seeing a wide-open space of green that they had all spent hours running around in but today a very different, far more exciting sight greeted them.

The amount of trucks and vans seemed to have more than doubled and now the field had been completely engulfed by people and transport. A huge stage, which had a massive black roof and powerful looking spotlights at the front as well as a grey backdrop and a sole microphone in the centre of it, had been built at the school end of the field and what could only be referred to as a 'pen' had been put up in front of it. There were the mats from the PE cupboard that were usually used for gymnastics for the younger ones to sit on and the benches that year 6 were allowed to use in assembly for them at the back. Filing into the pen, Sophie looked away from the stage behind the barriers. There were lines of cameras and people attaching things, removing things and building things on them in an effort to get the perfect view of what was to come. Cameramen were climbing over each other, poking each other in the eye or standing on other people's fingers just to be the one with a clear shot.

All around the fence that circled the field, local residents and people from further afield had gathered on ladders to peer over and see what all the fuss was about. Mr Houghton, who was now at the front of the stage, was pointing to where he wanted each class to sit. The teachers who were supposed to be making sure that all the children who might shout out and disrupt were on the ends of rows so that they could be dragged out at a moment's notice, were also getting distracted by what was happening around them and so children were basically sitting wherever they wanted to.

Finally reaching their positions on the benches, the year sixes took their seats. In front of them was the rest of the school, with the new Foundation Stage children, who were mostly still not bothered at having to leave their parents, sitting at the front like meerkats in an effort to see the absolutely nothing that was happening on stage. Yasmine and Sophie had fought their way back through the line and had ended up in the middle of the class, right in the centre, to look at the stage. Katie shuffled down from where she was and the three friends sat together. The enormity of the stage hit home once they had sat down. It looked more like something set up at a rock concert than in a school field. Only the most famous, richest, cleverest man on Earth could warrant something as extraordinary as this.

Through the mutterings of confusion from everyone, Mrs Tabard walked herself onto the stage, took the microphone out and screeched at one of the year threes and silence descended across the entire field and beyond.

'Cameron, you've forgotten your lunchbox. Your mum has dropped it off and I've left it in the classroom.'

Everyone turned to stare at Cameron, who was turning bright red and not taking his eyes off Mrs Tabard.

'Thank you,' said Cameron in an extremely sheepish manner, knowing that everyone was staring at him and knew that he would be having sandwiches for dinner.

It took a few seconds for everyone to stop looking before Mr Houghton rescued Cameron by taking the microphone off Mrs Tabard, 'OK, thank you, Mrs Tabard.'

Mrs Tabard simply raised her hand in acknowledgement and didn't even look back as she pottered off. She had new-year permission slips to sort, and nothing was going to stop her. *One day* she thought to herself, *one day I will teach a class*!

Mr Houghton cleared his throat and put down his cup of tea in his 'Best Teacher' mug that someone had bought him as a present at the end of last year. 'Well good morning, everyone.'

'Good morning, Mr Houghton, good morning, everyone,' all the children (and some of the film crews) replied in perfect monotonous unison as they did every day. It sounded ridiculous.

'We have had some great honours and experiences in the past here at Pinkleton Primary, but this, children, might be the greatest of those honours. At the end of last year, I, along with hundreds of other head teachers, was invited to enter a top-secret competition organised by Shadow.'

The excitement grew but Sophie wondered how a competition entered by hundreds could be top secret.

'I was given the challenge of convincing the people at Shadow that our school would be the best place for their team to unveil a brand-new product. I have spent the last few months preparing presentations, writing letters, taking photos trying to get evidence ready that says our school is amazing. A few weeks later, I heard back from them saying that our school would be perfect for such an event and that we had won.'

The excitement grew more…

'So here we are, Shadow has invited the world's media and viewers all over the planet to come to our school to hear what they have to say. I have absolutely no idea what the announcement is…'

Sophie also doubted that as she could hear a slight change in his tone.

'…but, without further ado, it gives me great pleasure, in fact, it is an honour, to introduce the man behind Shadow and inventions such as the self-driving car and the Internet Implant – Mr Alton King…'

The children finally exploded with excitement. Screams and shouting engulfed the field and the lights on all the cameras turned on. Reporters at the back of the children started narrating to camera where they were and what was happening to the millions of people who were tuning in to watch the news. Sophie, Yasmine and Katie stood on the benches in order to get a better view of the man many viewed as the greatest man on the planet.

From behind the curtain at the back of the stage, Alton King emerged like a vampire from a coffin. He quite simply glided, effortlessly, to the front of the stage. It was as if he was on wheels. Over his matchstick-like shoulders was draped a long blue coat that could have doubled as a cloak. His face was pale; he looked as if he had been kissed by death himself and brought back from the abyss. A skinny, protruding, pointy nose left his face behind by some distance and on top of it sat a pair of circular, rimless glasses that must have served some purpose but were surely too far from his eyes to work as actual glasses. With just wisps of hair around his ears, the light would have reflected off the top of him had it not been for the sheer white of his head. This was a man who very rarely left the house or the office. Sophie chuckled to herself as she wondered, based on his complexion, whether he was an actual vampire or other nocturnal mythical creature that used to come out only at night. She didn't share the joke with her two friends as they wouldn't appreciate it nearly as much as she did.

Arriving at the front of the stage, King removed his coat and hung it on the back of the chair that had been left for him. Underneath his coat, he was wearing a black jumper and a pair of grey trousers. Weirdly, on his feet was a pair of bright blue trainers - this was a man who clearly did not and would not exercise even if his life depended on it (which it looked like it might do).

King raised one hand in the air in acknowledgement of the cheers and lowered it almost immediately. The crowd fell silent. The respect he commanded was jaw-dropping. No one on the field or watching at home was shocked by the frail appearance of the world's cleverest man. He had been all over the news and technology sites since the Internet Implant had launched all those years ago. It was common knowledge that King was eccentric and more than a little unusual – he never allowed anyone into his factory at Shadow HQ, he worked completely alone and the people around the world were so grateful to him for the developments he had made, that they all respected his desire for privacy and so never bothered him. People put his pale complexion down to him working long hours in dimly lit rooms; in an effort to make the world a better place, he had sacrificed his health and his image. As a result, he was worshipped as a hero who had given up so much to help the human race advance since the olden days had finished and the mythicals had left, freeing up humans from worrying about attack or incident.

'Thank you,' King said coldly as he picked up the microphone that was left in the stand by Mr Houghton. Year 6 sat back on the benches and waited with anticipation to find out why he was there. Not least Sophie, Yasmine and Katie.

'I imagine you are all wondering why I have called a press conference at a primary school in the middle of the country with very little warning or indication as to what it is about.'

King spoke with such delicate tones that nobody really noticed that he wasn't that good at public speaking, and he was in fact not great in front of an audience.

'Well, I bring good news from Shadow. For decades our world was stalked by unimaginable mythical monsters. We faced grave threats daily: aliens, ghosts, outrageous beasts, they all came to do us harm but those days are now long gone. Technology is now in a place whereby we live fantastic lives not facing the threats of yesterday – dealing with evils from all walks of the imagination, losing friends and relatives because of the tribulations of sharing our world with monsters…'

Sophie was excited because this was the most she had ever heard someone talk about the mythicals in front of a large crowd before, so she carried on listening attentively.

'…It now gives me great pleasure to announce that I have received word that practically every person over the age of 11 in the developed world does now in fact own an Internet Implant. With secondary school children going back to school all over the country all receiving their new present free, every human in recognised countries at secondary school age and over now has total, uninterrupted access to everything they could ever wish for.'

The crowd clapped and cheered enthusiastically. Sophie looked around at everyone. They were all happy, except for Miss Sissins, who looked to be confused and looking around for something.

'This has left me in a bit of a quandary,' King continued.

This word left most of the children at Pinkleton Primary a bit lost. Sophie whispered to Katie and Yasmine that it just meant that he didn't know what to do but both of them looked at her displeased that she had assumed they didn't know what it meant.

King continued to float around the stage, very slowly; his posh, well-spoken accent was soothing all those around him, almost sending them to sleep, yet the message he was delivering had all their interests peaked.

'After a few months of thinking about where to take my company next, I have decided to create something that would benefit the members of the population that are always so difficult to please with my next project.'

A few children, Sophie included, seemed to work out who he was talking about and smiled at each other.

'I'm talking about... children.'

That was what Sophie thought he was going to say. She stared at Katie and Yasmine in disbelief. They just stared back also before clapping incessantly like seals. Sophie wondered if she could read King's next thought and unveil the exact thing that she had been ranting to her dad about just last night.

Chapter 4 - Infinite Possibilities

'The children of today are the greatest assets on this planet; they are the fortunate generation for they have not had to grow up facing the threats that we adults did and for too long they have been ignored by too many people. I intend to change all that with the grand unveiling of this...'

King took a remote control out of his pocket and pressed a button. From behind the curtain came a child-sized dummy on wheels. On top of its head was what looked like a spider's web; it covered the part of the dummy's head that would have had hair and had bright flashing lights on the ends.

'This,' King continued 'is the Internet Implant for kids. It will be used by children as their passage onto the immersive internet. Now I know it doesn't look like much at the moment...' King walked behind the dummy and put his hands on its shoulders, '...but this is just a prototype designed to implant the implant. The actual chip for inside the child's head is this.' King took a small round, white ball out of his pocket and held it up. The majority of the crowd squinted to try and see what he was holding but only a few could actually make it out.

'Once implanted, the implant will shrink down to microscopic size and will not be visible to the naked eye. However, should the child wish to take it out, they can do and while it is being removed, it will grow back to the size you see before you so that it doesn't get lost.'

The children in the crowd all looked at each other in disbelief. It was happening. Sophie continued glancing at Miss Sissins, who was again looking around herself and appearing rather worried. Sophie tried to catch her eye but couldn't.

'There will of course be limitations in what children can access but, on the whole, they too will be able to communicate with anyone else on the planet in a matter of nanoseconds or browse for any fact or piece of information they desire – dependent on their parent's permission. We can't just let these children loose online with all the dangers the internet presents.'

Mr Houghton could be seen nodding vigorously at this; he was a strong supporter of internet safety – as any head teacher should be.

'They will though be able to watch any film, read any story or visit any place their heart desires all without leaving the comfort of their own settee or bedroom.'

King continued with the children of Pinkleton Primary in a complete trance, hypnotised by what he was saying, all around the world as well, children were glued to their devices excited at the fact that they were going to be given the same opportunity as the adults.

'It has been a long process but, after all those months of research and development, I am very pleased to announce that we will be implanting the first five lucky children with their own implant here today at Pinkleton Primary School.'

At this, the pen of children erupted. Cheers, whoops and screams dominated the air. Film crews were clapping as they tried to imagine what it would be like to be the first parent of the first child implanted. Parents standing on ladders leaning against the fence around the field were shouting their children's names in an effort to get them picked.

King again raised his hand and lowered it. Quiet descended and children started biting their crossed fingers in anticipation. King clicked his fingers and Mr Houghton wheeled out the large red chair that was normally kept in his office.

King continued to explain, even more relaxed than he had been, 'I don't want anyone to worry, this will be a completely painless experience and the recipient will walk away today with access to a universe-sized library of information.'

One child, who Sophie guessed must have been in about year 5, screamed, 'Pick me!'

King finally smiled the tiniest smile you could ever see as he could sense the excitement on the field even if he wasn't caught up in it.

'Now, first of all, I would like to invite up,' the children gasped as King paused for what felt like an age... 'Yasmine Ariti from year 6'

Sophie and Katie turned to look at their friend. Yasmine was simply staring forward while hundreds of eyes of the younger children turned to stare at her – it took a split-second for the clapping and cheering to start but when they did the whistles and the cheering almost deafened Sophie, Yasmine and Katie who were still gawping, open-mouthed. Yasmine was to be the first of the chosen ones.

Eventually, Sophie put her hand on Yasmine's shoulder and whispered, 'Go on then!' with an air of frightened excitement.

Dazed, Yasmine raised herself slowly and began to walk towards the end of the line of benches and onwards to the stage. Within a matter of seconds, Yasmine had gone from an unknown 10-year-old sat in school on the first day of year 6, to having her name broadcast to anyone on the planet that was watching this world-changing event. Her name would trend on social media, people would love her, people would be jealous of her and people would hate her but none of that entered Yasmine's mind as she began to ascend the steps onto the stage.

'If you could simply sit yourself here please Miss Ariti.' King gestured towards the chair from Mr Houghton's office.

Oblivious, Yasmine just stared forwards at the crowd and didn't do or say anything. Eventually, Mr Houghton put his hand on her shoulder, led her to the chair and sat Yasmine down on it; she held onto the arms tightly and continued staring straight ahead. A smile was beginning to creep across her face, as the enormity of what was about to happen began to sink in. Cameras flashed and all over the world people were watching the first *child* ever be given access.

'Okay Yasmine, I'm simply going to place this device on your head, there will be a quick jolt, like a pinprick, in the left side of your head, and then you will be good to go straight away,' King explained, reassuringly.

Yasmine finally turned her gaze from the crowd, looked at King, and nodded. 'When you're finished, could you stand over there next to your head teacher.'

Mr Houghton waved as if to say *yes, I'm still here, don't forget me.*

'It may be slightly overwhelming at first but all you need to do is look at the crowd normally and then you should be back and in control. It will take some getting used to but I cannot stress enough that it is perfectly safe.'

Yasmine nodded again. No one had ever really seen Yasmine speechless; she always had something to say and normally said it quite loudly. This was quite a novelty for everyone.

'Are you ready, Miss?' King asked. At the back of the crowd, Yasmine could see her mum and dad watching on proudly – well her dad was clearly zoned out on his implant talking to a business colleague about some deal, but finally he zoned back in after receiving a jab from Yasmine's mum and his gaze returned to his daughter. He gave her the thumbs up from behind the pen and Yasmine smiled a huge smile. She was ready.

Sophie watched as King placed the cap on Yasmine's head. The lights began to light up and King pressed another button on his remote. The lights on the headset flicked between green and blue for about five seconds, Yasmine then jolted slightly to her right as what must have been the pinprick sensation went through her head. Five seconds later, every light was green and King was removing the cap and making sure Yasmine was ok.

'How did that feel?' he asked cautiously.

'Fine,' Yasmine replied, slightly out of it.

'How does it feel now?' King continued.

'A little unusual: if I look straight ahead, I can see the crowd, if I look, kind of into thin air in front of where my focus is, I can see white,' Yasmine explained.

'That's excellent,' King replied, almost sounding relieved, but as he did so he seemed to look over at someone in the crowd near Miss Sissins and shake his head sombrely. Sophie looked over again at Miss Sissins and saw her shake her head too.

'Take your place over there next to Mr Houghton.'

Yasmine walked towards him, he put his hand on her arm to help her balance and there Yasmine stood, at that moment, the most famous girl in the world.

Sophie was slightly frustrated. After the argument she had with her dad last night, she thought she deserved one. She was delighted for her friend of course but Sophie was understandably a bit jealous as well. Katie also was sat down on the bench downhearted.

'What's wrong?' Sophie asked.

'They clearly need your parents to sign off on you having one. They aren't going to get my dad to give permission, are they?' Katie replied in a tone that was aggressive but not aimed at Sophie.

Sophie was about to reply when King started speaking again. It was time for the second lucky child to step forward.

'Reuben, in year 4,' King announced.

The whole school looked baffled.

'Reuben in year 4?' one of the year 6 boys scoffed, 'Who's Reuben in year 4?'

No one had ever heard of a Reuben in year 4. Pinkleton was small enough for everyone to know everybody else and no one knew who it was; children were looking around their group asking if anyone else had heard of such an imposter. No one came forward.

Even Mrs Tabard, who had finished counting the dinner money and was now on the prowl for someone to run the healthy tuck shop at break time, shouted, 'Who?' and she knew everybody!

After looking around all the children in school, Sophie noticed Mr Houghton with a huge grin on his face, standing on the stage; he was eagerly beckoning towards someone in the crowd.

'Come on Reuben, where are you?' King asked.

'I think you might have the wrong name, we don't have a Reuben here,' Ryan Myers shouted out, desperate to point out the mistake that had apparently been made.

Sophie continued watching Mr Houghton, he was still gesturing for someone only known to him to come up to the stage.

'Reuben, Reuben Houghton,' King was beginning to get a bit agitated.

'Reuben... Houghton' Sophie muttered to herself.

She wasn't alone. Mr Houghton had often spoken about a son of his being his pride and joy but had always said he was extremely happy at the school he was at in the next village. Sophie decided there could only be one reason that he would even think about moving him. Meanwhile, on stage, Mr Houghton was beginning to get quite agitated. He had blatantly enrolled his son at school so he could have him on the list for an implant and everyone watching was beginning to realise this as well. Had Yasmine not still been a bit dazed, she would be the first to express the lack of fairness in this!

Eventually, a short, blonde-reddish-haired boy stood up from in the middle of the year 4 line and turned to face his admiring crowd. Sophie looked at him and couldn't see a resemblance between Reuben and his dad at all. He waved aggressively and started to bow. Unbeknown to Reuben, the only people cheering were those that were oblivious to the fact that the boy had never been seen at school before - mostly the film crews and people beyond the fence that surrounded the school, who weren't allowed in.

At the same time, the teachers and other adults in and around the scene who knew what was happening were looking at Mr Houghton. He now had sweat patches on his shirt under his arms due to the threatening glares he was receiving from the knowing people in the crowd.

Clapping slowed around the field as it became clear exactly what was going on. The camera operators and the other new people started to notice that none of the children or the parents were clapping and so their applause started to peter out. It was starting to sound more like one of those slow claps of annoyance and frustration.

The head and his son had fiddled the system and the whole world was beginning to see it. Reuben continued his walk with huge pride. The sense of dread that Sophie guessed he had had when his name was announced had clearly gone and the shock was obviously not affecting him at all; he was now waving vigorously to a crowd who really weren't waving back, no one responded and by now it was becoming a farce.

That was until one lone voice shouted, 'Good luck Reuben, my sweet. You deserve it!'

The whole crowd turned to get a glimpse of who this was. Towards the back of the cameras and film crews stood a woman wearing sunglasses and a flowery dress, waving like a lunatic.

'Thanks, mummy!' Reuben shouted back, suddenly filled with even more confidence at the sight of his beloved mother. The adults around the school looked up at Mr Houghton again, this time with a look of contempt but also a look of *we know exactly what you've done.*

Reuben reached centre stage. He walked straight over to the microphone stand where King was still standing and took the microphone out of King's hand. King looked at him in disbelief then shot Mr Houghton a disgusted look. The look of embarrassment on Mr Houghton's face disappeared temporarily and he glared angrily back at King. Sophie swore she was the only one to see this.

Whilst the two of them were exchanging evil glances, Reuben had started a speech, whether it was pre-prepared or not was anybody's guess.

'If I could just say a few words before this amazing honour is bestowed upon me,' Reuben began in an incredibly posh voice.

Sophie thought he sounded like he should have been at one of those private boarding schools and Ryan Myers in particular was licking his lips at this new fresh meat that he could get his teeth into!

Reuben continued, 'I am extremely humbled to be accepting this as one of Pinklegram Primary's most loved students.'

At the side, Mr Houghton seemed to cough and say 'Pinkleton' at the same time, spotting his son's problem with the unit of measurement at the end of the village name and trying to help him save face (especially from Ryan who was beginning to crack his knuckles in anticipation).

'I have not been here long…'

'Yeah, about half an hour,' said Mrs Tabard, not very quietly!

'…but I already feel like the school have accepted me and hopefully, I can help *us* improve with my far superior intelligence and ability. I look forward to working with all of you as much as I'm sure you will enjoy working with me,' Reuben bowed.

There was one solitary clap from Reuben's mum in sunglasses towards the back. Everyone else sat there, stone-faced.

'OK, right, err, well, that, was, err… unexpected,' King said uncomfortably. King was seen by many as being uncomfortable a lot of the time but this was just plain weird and awkward.

After a few seconds for Reuben to get comfy and announce that he was ready, King gave the exact same spiel he gave to Yasmine a few minutes ago and placed the cap on Reuben's head. This time there was no whooping or celebrating. It wasn't Reuben's fault his dad had abused his position and he had 'cheated' his way to getting an implant. Although, it kind of was Reuben's fault that he had been a real arrogant, ego-centric buffoon on his way up to the stage. Also, the children, especially the likes of Katie, who knew she was going to miss out, couldn't help but feel angry.

The rest of the process carried off exactly like it had done before with Yasmine. The lights flashed green and Reuben stood up slowly. His mum clapped ferociously and Mr Houghton patted him on the back. The expressions on the faces of the children were priceless; they had been cheated and they knew it. If Reuben was still going to be here tomorrow, he would certainly now be of interest to Ryan.

These thoughts didn't linger long with the children though as King said, 'Lucky person number three then...' The children immediately forgot about the injustice they had just witnessed and began to murmur about who would be next. Every child in school again sat bolt upright with arms folded and legs crossed, hoping against all the odds that it would be them. Silence fell and King temporarily played on the tension by looking around the crowd and dragging out the announcement as long as he could.

'Year 6 again...' King started, 'Sophie Hardy'.

Chapter 5 - Sophie's Go

Sophie said nothing and just stared forwards. She didn't move a muscle. On the surface it looked like nothing had happened to her and that she was just another member of the crowd that sat aghast. Underneath her calm exterior though, her brain had gone into overdrive with a mix of excitement, questions and outrageous thoughts. Why had she been picked? Could her parents have had a word with the right person after their argument yesterday? Would this make her popular with her friends or would they stop talking to her?

She must have only been like this for about ten seconds, but her brain had never tried to process so much information in one go; it was like her life was flashing in front of her, searching for an experience she had been through that could help her out. The problem wasn't that there was nothing to help, there was so much compared to most 10-year-olds – Falling out with her parents last night, Clara moving away a few weeks ago, living with very little money and just 'getting by' in their high-off-the-ground house. All of these memories tried to help Sophie, but her brain was having none of it. She was dumbfounded, thunderstruck and flabbergasted all in one go and even all the stories of mythicals from yesteryear her dad had told her did nothing to help.

Sophie felt a jab on her arm and heard the voice of Katie in her ear. 'Go on then!' she was whispering through gritted teeth.

Hearing that, Sophie partly snapped back into the real world and started to take in her surroundings. It felt like the whole school was looking at her. In actuality, the whole entire world was looking at the latest lucky child, but that thought was still out of reach of Sophie's brain for now. As Sophie stood up, a louder cheer emanated from the crowd outside the gate and, before she knew it, the whole school was in rapturous applause. Sophie was well-known and well-liked by all, and most of the children and staff couldn't think of anyone better to get an implant if it wasn't going to be them.

Sophie shuffled down the line of year sixes and looked up as she reached the end. When she did, she caught the glance of one of the teachers. Miss Sissins was the only person not clapping or cheering, she appeared decidedly frightened with a stern look that Sophie had never seen before. She looked worried and was simply staring, almost apologetically at Sophie and looked like a statue that was breathing deeply. Had Sophie been a bit more with it, she would have asked her what was wrong, but she was on another level of emotion and couldn't begin to comprehend how to ask a question never mind understand what the answer might be. Within a few seconds, she had forgotten everything that had just happened and felt like she was gliding to the stage at the front, not in control of her own legs. She levitated up the stairs and floated over to King, who shook her hand.

His handshake was unrealistically tight to say he was greeting a ten-year-old and appeared so frail. At one point, Sophie thought he was actually trying to hurt her. On closer inspection, Sophie noticed that King was even paler in real life and his eyes were a lot more tired looking than Sophie could have realised from being far away from him in the crowd. His skin was hanging off his face, almost as if it didn't fit properly. King started to give out the same instructions he had given the other two and invited Sophie to sit down.

As Sophie sat, a few more of her brain cells came back to reality and started to almost work properly again. This allowed her to see two people far off in the crowd who were standing arm in arm. Sophie's focus came back completely and she could see that it was her mum and dad. Mum had her sunglasses on and her head on dad's shoulder and dad had his arm around mum almost like he was holding her up. They looked extremely happy and extremely proud and they both gave Sophie a subtle wave and Sophie waved back. Sophie's sister – Lizzie - was sat in the pram, fast asleep with her cuddly giraffe.

'Is that ok with you, Sophie?' said a voice.

Sophie's final brain function came back properly and she realised that King had finished the instruction.

'Err, yes,' Sophie replied, guessing the instructions had been the same as they had been for Yasmine and Reuben and so just agreed without thinking.

Sophie scanned the stage. Yasmine was standing there staring into space, probably enjoying the Internet Implant experience straight away as she stood there, basking in newfound knowledge. Reuben and Mr Houghton were standing next to her both looking smug with Mr Houghton waving excitedly to the crowd. Then there was King, who was just staring at Sophie, right in her face. His eyes were piercing and made Sophie want to just say 'yes'. In his wrinkly fingers was the machine that Sophie had seen used on Yasmine and Reuben. Up close, it looked like a jellyfish with blue fingertips. Before Sophie could study anymore, King started the process of plugging Sophie in. As he placed the contraption on her head, Sophie heard a shout from somewhere.

'NO! DON'T! THE LIGHTS AREN'T RIGHT!'

Sophie tried to process where it had come from but couldn't. She scanned around the crowd and saw Miss Sissins fighting her way to the front. It dawned on her that something wasn't as it should have been. She looked for her mum and dad again. They weren't hugging anymore - Amelia had her hands over her mouth and Tom had his hands on his head. Sophie heard a loud witch-like cackle from next to her but, before she could turn to see who it was, King was attaching the machine over her head. His eyes had gone from tired to fiery orange. Flames danced in his irises and veins pulsated in the side of his head.

'She'll be fine. This is what we *need* to happen!' he almost chortled.

Sophie couldn't move as the machine turned on. It stung so much like someone was stabbing her with a thousand pins. The pain didn't last long though. Although it hurt so much, Sophie was distracted by something else and the pain stopped.

All around her, everything had turned black; it was like someone had just flicked the lights off and plunged her into darkness. There were though, flashes of lightning-like electricity bouncing off invisible walls in her eyes, like when there's a thunderstorm at night. Sophie felt petrified yet was managing to keep her cool. She breathed deeply, trying to regain her composure. Deep breath, count, deep breath, count. Opening her eyes gradually, she was met with the gaze of a pair of ocean-blue eyes immediately in front of her. These eyes were there for no longer than a lightning strike, but Sophie made them out as clear as day. Seconds later, another strike and Sophie caught sight of the eyes again. She knew them from somewhere, but they looked different compared to how they normally looked meaning Sophie couldn't place them. Another strike and Sophie saw more. Jet-black hair was brushed forward almost covering the person's face, and then the hair turned red and the eyes green for a few nanoseconds before switching back to black and blue. *That isn't right*, Sophie thought to herself. That hair, with those eyes, it's usually tied up in a ponytail. Another flash and it became clear who Sophie was seeing in the electric flashes. It was her cousin, Clara.

Now that Sophie had worked out what she was dealing with and who she was facing, she began to work out when the flashes would come by counting the seconds between them and she would try to make out Clara in more detail.

Flash – Clara was clearly in a mess – her hair was all over the place and her eyes looked exhausted and stressed. Her hair and eyes kept changing to different colours though, almost like they couldn't decide who they wanted to be.

Flash – Clara was on some kind of mattress unable to move. Her hands and feet had been strapped down.

Flash – Clara was mouthing something.

Sophie concentrated unbelievably hard, staring at Clara whenever she appeared, reading her lips to try and make out what she was saying. After about three more flashes, Sophie had deciphered what it was.

'Get me out of here,' Sophie said to herself.

'How?' Sophie mimed back. It seemed to fall on deaf ears though as Clara just carried on uttering the same five words over and over, almost as if Sophie could see Clara, but Clara couldn't see her.

Sophie looked around herself for what she could do next. With a jolt, Clara's face became more distorted, and Sophie could see less of her with each flash. The surroundings started to get lighter and before she realised what was going on, she was blinded by a bright light.

'GET ME OUT OF HERE!' Sophie shouted as she woke up. She was greeted by a face that made her scream again but much more quietly – Mrs Tabard, who was now doubling up as the school's first aider, had a wet paper towel in her hand and was mopping Sophie's forehead letting the water run into her eyes.

Sophie tried to sit up but struggled. She took in her surroundings and realised she was lying on the floor in the classroom with her feet up on a chair. Around her were Mrs Tabard, Yasmine, Katie, Amelia and Tom.

'See! I told you she didn't need an ambulance!' Mrs Tabard said, clearly aiming her exclamation at Sophie's parents.

A huge sigh of relief was had by all in the room. Sophie lay back down again but didn't want to close her eyes. Who knew where she would end up if she did so?

Chapter 6 – An Explanation

A few minutes after waking, Sophie was sitting up and talking. Her mum and dad had left the room to ring her Nan to say that she was ok. She had seen what happened on the internet and desperately wanted reassurance that what she had seen hadn't done Sophie any harm. Sophie of course had no idea what had happened to her. No one could have seen what she had and she wondered what it must have looked like to everyone else. Fortunately, now that Mrs Tabard had gone off with Sophie's parents for a quick chat and Miss Sissins was stood just outside the classroom door with her arms folded across her chest and her hand over her mouth (clearly contemplating something deep), Sophie was free to share her experience with Yasmine and Katie and find out what they had seen.

'What happened?' the three girls all said together.

'You first,' Sophie got in before anyone else had the chance to speak.

Neither of the other two said anything. Katie just walked over to the class computer and loaded up a video site. She clicked on a video and up came a news feed which had been broadcasting the announcement. It clearly showed Sophie being asked to sit down by King and him going to put the machine on Sophie's head. In the process of that happening, someone had shouted and Sophie could make out Miss Sissins trying to get to the front and a few people screaming. When the implantation machine was placed on Sophie's head, she fell off the chair onto the floor. The arms of the machine hadn't turned green or blue as they had with Yasmine and Reuben, they had turned red and green. Sophie lay motionless on the floor and carnage had ensued. Some people were running towards the stage, other people were running from it. Cameramen were refocusing their cameras to get the best shot and reporters had started to adlib what it was they were seeing for the millions of people watching at home. After that, the video stopped.

'Then Mr Houghton and Miss Sissins carried you in here, to get you out of sight,' Yasmine explained, 'you woke up about half an hour after you had blanked out.'

'Half an hour! It only felt like a few seconds,' Sophie replied.

'No, we were all sitting around for a while waiting for you to come back,' Yasmine concluded.

Katie hadn't said anything, and, while this wasn't unusual for her, Sophie couldn't help but wonder that there might be something a bit more to it.

So, she asked, 'Are you ok?'

Katie nodded not very convincingly.

'Sure?' Sophie continued.

'You're famous,' Katie finally said, rather flippantly.

'Pardon?' Sophie replied, adjusting her position so that she was sat at the table as you would expect in a lesson.

'You're name and face are all over the internet, the whole world watched you become the third child to get an implant but the first person ever to have it fail. You're everywhere. All of the press that was outside is now waiting at the school door to get a photo or an interview with you!' Katie continued with arms folded.

Momentarily forgetting about the Clara situation, a realisation hit Sophie. Of course, she was now known to everyone. The announcement of her name before she went up on stage had made her famous, now that she had fainted as well, she would be infamous. The school that she went to, major aspects of her life had been broadcast to everyone. The thought scared Sophie.

Yasmine looked like she was staring into space again; she was clearly accessing her implant, 'Yes, your name is all over the internet. Major news sites, social media, everywhere. You're the most famous 10-year-old on the planet at the minute!'

Just then the classroom door opened and Miss Sissins walked in; she still had her arms folded and spoke, rather abruptly, to the girls.

'Girls, give us a minute please,' she said, aiming it at Yasmine and Katie.

'But…' Yasmine started to say as Miss Sissins gave her a glance that let her know she was serious. She didn't give the look often, normally only when someone had done something outrageous at school, but the girls had seen it before and knew she meant it. Respecting her as they did, the girls hugged Sophie and left.

'You need to tell us what happened to *you*,' Yasmine tried to say but Miss Sissins closed the door behind them while she was mid-sentence.

Sophie could still see the pair of them in the corridor talking to her mum and dad.

'What did she say?' Miss Sissins said without the hint of a smile.

Sophie gave her a completely blank look. Normally she would trust Miss Sissins with anything but there was something about her manner that wasn't normal.

'Sophie, what did Clara say to you?' she said ever so slightly louder and firmer.

This really took Sophie aback. How did she know? Did she trust her to tell her the truth about this? No, Sophie decided, not yet, not when she was acting like this.

'I don't know what you mean,' Sophie lied.

'When you passed out,' Miss Sissins began, 'you saw Clara and she gave you a message, what was it? Exactly? Word for word?'

Sophie continued to plead ignorance. This teacher who she looked up to and admired and loved being taught by was beginning to scare her.

'I don't know!' Sophie implored, fighting back her emotions.

'Don't lie to me,' Miss Sissins was getting nasty now.

Sophie was about to launch another appeal of her innocence but was saved by the classroom door opening. Her parents had come to get her.

'We're taking her home,' Amelia said calmly, 'it's been a busy day.'

Miss Sissins changed back to her normal, jolly self, 'OK, Amelia. Now you make sure you're back in tomorrow Soph, as we have even more exciting things to do tomorrow,' she then glared at Sophie when she knew her mum and dad couldn't see her.

'She'll be in,' Tom started, 'but there has been enough excitement for one day. I'm sure you'll take care of her though Miss Sissins. She does love being in your class.'

'I'll take care of her,' Miss Sissins replied and she looked at Sophie in such a way that Sophie wanted to scream but, she kept it in. She was tough and wasn't going to let her see she was getting to her.

'Where's Lizzie?' Sophie asked her mum and dad.

'Your nan came to fetch her a few minutes ago. I might go and get her later if this calms down a bit,' Tom replied.

After collecting her bag, Sophie and her parents left the classroom and headed out towards the cesspit of reporters that were waiting at the school's main entrance.

'Sophie, we need you to prepare yourself,' Tom started to say.

'What for?' asked Sophie clinging to her parents tightly.

'Well,' Tom began again, 'seeing as the entire press conference was broadcast to billions of people all over the world, you are now, how do I put this, quite well known and various people would like to know what happened from your point of view.'

Although Yasmine and Katie had let her know this already, Sophie thought it might get them into trouble if she admitted they had told her and so decided to keep that from her parents, 'What does that mean?' she asked innocently.

Before either parent could answer her, Mr Houghton appeared in the corridor with Reuben standing next to him, looking decidedly cross.

'They're everywhere,' Mr Houghton said looking extremely pleased with himself, more so than he probably should, given that one of his students had just fainted in full view of the whole world.

'Haven't they left yet?' Amelia asked, hugging Sophie even more tightly than she had been before.

'No, they're all still outside, clambering for an interview with Sophie,' Mr Houghton replied. He had this huge smile on his face as if he was enjoying seeing the world's media focused on the school.

At this point, Reuben was still looking cross and looked like he was trying to stare Sophie out. Sophie, on the other hand, was having none of it and simply looked through him.

'They're calling you 'The Singularity' because no one has ever seen anyone react like that to the implantation process,' Mr Houghton said to Sophie.

Sophie thought about what he'd said, she hadn't seen the adult implantation process before; she had read about it and from what she had read it seemed to follow a similar procedure and had also never heard of anything like that happening to anyone.

Reuben finally piped up, 'Some of them are calling you 'The Glitch'. I think that's much more accurate,' he said it all through gritted teeth in the corner of his mouth. He was clearly put out by all of the focus that Sophie was getting.

'Where's Alton King, he should be able to help get rid of some of the attention?' Tom asked.

'He ran off as soon as Sophie was cleared off the stage,' Mr Houghton added, 'and the entrance hall is crammed with journalists and so is the hill leading up to school. You're going to have to go through them. If you need any help with what to say then I can talk to them for you.'

'What about the police? Can't they help get us out?' Amelia asked, starting to look desperate with worry for her poor girl.

Ears suddenly pricked with interest, Reuben lost his stare at Sophie and said with huge smugness, 'Oh, King was very adamant that the police *not* be involved. No crime has been committed.'

Sophie looked at him carefully. She was starting to think that Reuben was jealous of the attention she was getting.

The Hardys then looked at each other. There was only one thing for it, they would have to barge their way through and get to the car that mum and dad had driven to school. None of them liked the idea of fighting their way through a barrage of questions and flailing microphones but they were going to have to. With that thought in mind, Tom and Amelia gripped Sophie's hands incredibly tightly as any parent would. The door to the main entrance was swung open by Amelia and the trio marched forward.

Lights flashed, chatter turned to shouting and Sophie felt extremely claustrophobic. She did her very best to block out everything around her but some things got through.

'How did it feel Sophie?'

'What happened, Sophie?'

'How does it feel to be famous all over the world?'

Lots more questions were shouted in Sophie's direction but she just held on incredibly tightly to her dad. Mum was in front but still holding Sophie's other hand, clearing a path as best she could.

The sheer number of bodies and the pressure began to take their toll on Amelia, she slipped slightly and just shouted, 'Can you please give my daughter some space, she's still in shock at what happened.'

Some of the reporters took note of this and held back their questions but others pounced on this opportunity to ask *their* questions. Sophie just wanted to scream and make it all stop but, being as determined as she was, she didn't, she knuckled down and forced herself through it.

Eventually, Amelia reached the car, opened the back door and dad bundled Sophie inside. Sophie strapped herself in and Tom did his best to shut the door. After a few goes and a few reporters' feet getting in the way, he managed it and got into the driver's seat. They sped off down the school driveway to the sanctuary of home.

In the back of the car, Sophie had very quickly come to realise that being famous wasn't great. She wasn't like a superhero with a secret identity. The whole planet had seen this happen to her. She was a household name now. From now on, no matter how much she would will it not to, this morning would always be a part of her and this frightened Sophie immensely. She would always be 'The Glitch' or 'The Singularity'. She was tough; there was no doubt about that. With all the experience she'd had in her short life, Sophie knew that she couldn't let this get the better of her. Clenching her fists, she thought about what she was going to do next. There was, in her eyes, only one thing for it – Yasmine and Katie needed telling about Clara.

Chapter 7 – The Morning After

One of the benefits of living in a tall block of flats was that nobody could get close enough to Sophie's window to take a photo like they potentially could in a regular house. One of the downsides was that there had been at least one helicopter circling the building all night.

The Hardys had arrived home to another mass gathering of reporters, some of which had gone straight to the flat after Sophie's 'event' had taken place and some of who had followed the Hardys home from school and waited outside. Sophie could remember her dad offering to hold her hand again on the way in but this time Sophie refused. She had gotten out of the car and walked in, straight-backed and proud of herself; she didn't need her dad to help her.

Sophie had fallen asleep on the settee not long after they had all got home. Her dad had covered her with a blanket and, as a result, she had spent all night in her school uniform. Waking up, Sophie rubbed her eyes and briefly forgot about what had happened to her.

'Is Lizzie still at Nan's?' was Sophie's first question upon seeing her mum.

'Yes, she stayed there for the night,' came the response, 'we thought she would be better out of the way, although Nan has had some reporters outside her house as well!'

The incident from yesterday leapt back into her memory and Sophie then didn't need to ask which nan Lizzie was with or why. One of Sophie's nans lived in a retirement home and had struggled for years to remember things. Her dad had told her that her husband (his dad) had gone out to the shops some thirty or forty years ago and had never come back. Grandma had struggled ever since and had spent the last ten years just sitting in a home repeatedly saying that one day he was coming back. Sophie's Mum's mum on the other hand was very much a part of their lives and Sophie cared greatly for her.

Flicking on the television, Sophie scanned what was on. There was the normal early morning rubbish but with the added twist that photos of Sophie were showing up on all the channels. 'The Singularity' kept being mentioned by the people sitting on the large settees; they were throwing out random 'facts' about Sophie that they must have acquired from people at school - hardly any of which were true. Sophie was shocked though when one of them brought up the time she had fainted while practising the nativity in year 2; some of the newsreaders and 'experts' even debated whether the fainting then and fainting now were related! Somehow, Sophie couldn't see a link and went to change the channel.

She realised quite quickly that now she had a decision to make – she could sit around moping all day or she could go into school. The idea of facing Miss Sissins scared her a lot but as she saw yesterday she never did anything while other people were around and so logically wouldn't be a risk as long as school was busy. Besides, she had to let Yasmine and Katie know what had actually happened.

Before she turned the news channel off, Sophie caught sight of a different video taken from in the crowd yesterday. She watched it carefully. As she remembered, King was putting the machine on her head; you couldn't see his facial expression from that distance. Then after a split second of it being on her head, Sophie was on the floor. Like she saw yesterday, Miss Sissins was already halfway onto the stage before Sophie collapsed, why? Sophie wasn't sure but she kept watching. Yasmine had knelt down beside Sophie, as did Mr Houghton. From within the crowd, Katie had run forward between all the children and found herself on stage; Mr Houghton pulled her away from Sophie and led her off the stage to the side. As the action unfolded, Miss Sissins could be clearly seen telling everyone to get back from a position kneeling down next to Sophie. Meanwhile, King snatched the machine and left the stage. In the next few seconds, someone stood up in front of someone taking the video and nothing else could be made out.

Deciding that the video was offering up nothing dramatically new, Sophie went back to thinking about Clara. It had been six weeks since she had moved away, the last day of year 5 in fact. Nobody had any idea she was moving – they didn't make a card for her at school or even say a final goodbye in the last assembly. As far as Sophie was aware, nobody had seen her or heard from her since the last day of last year. They had even said 'goodbye' on the walk home that day with Sophie assuming that she would see Clara over the holiday but then later that evening the note had been passed.

'Mum, have you heard from Uncle Matthew and Uncle Josh since they moved?' Matthew Betts was Amelia's brother, he had married Uncle Josh a few years ago and the pair had adopted Clara as their only child when Clara was a new-born baby.

'No dear. Not sure if we'll hear from them any time soon,' she said honestly.

'Why?' Sophie asked.

'That's life dear, people move away.'

Sophie didn't think that sounded right. Yes, friends sometimes move away and you lose touch but not your brother!

'Have you been round to their house?' Sophie asked, doing her best to make sense of the situation.

'Yes dear, there's nobody there. They've moved away like they said so in their note. What would be the point in me going around there again?'

Amelia was making out that what she was saying was obvious, however, still not convinced, Sophie kept probing her, 'Have you video called them or tracked them?'

Amelia then emerged from the kitchen with breakfast on a tray. She looked at Sophie and gave a half-hearted smile, 'They're gone sweetie, their implants are turned off, and they clearly don't want to be found. I don't know what's happened but they said it was nothing personal in their note. They just wanted a new start.'

Sophie was hoping to be enlightened but was now more confused than ever. 'Can you drive me to school today so I don't have to walk please?' Sophie asked politely changing the subject.

'Are you sure you want to go in?' Tom asked, walking into the room ready for another day at the factory, 'you're the biggest news story that isn't about technology since the day the mythicals left!'

'You mean The Departure?' Sophie asked part excited, part petrified.

Mum was shocked at what she had just heard, 'Tom! Don't tell her that! You'll frighten the poor girl!'

Sophie knew that the day the mythicals all disappeared was known as 'The Departure' as no one knew exactly what had happened or why they had gone but she was intrigued by dad's last comment. The only other interesting thing that had happened that day, and Sophie knew to be completely unrelated, was that it was Clara's birthday.

'Well, yeah, I want to go in,' replied Sophie, 'I'm not sitting around here all day watching myself on the news. I may as well go. Anyway, you told Miss Sissins I would be.'

'I think we need to talk about what happened,' Tom suggested.

'There isn't a lot to tell,' Sophie lied, 'I just remember blacking out and waking up on the floor.' Sophie had given a lot of thought as to whether to tell her parents what was going on while she had travelled back in the car yesterday. She decided that until she knew more, she would keep it between herself and her friends. It wasn't that she didn't trust her mum and dad; it was just that they could stop her from doing something about it whereas her friends couldn't.

'There's something you aren't telling us...' Tom probed, 'you know you can tell us anything.'

Sophie looked at him blankly and tried really hard to hide the guilt she was feeling about lying to her dad. She decided that her parents had other things to worry about, never mind her daughter having visions!

'OK, I'll drive you,' Tom said, eventually.

'Can we pick up Yazz and Katie on the way?' Sophie asked.

'Their mums sent me a message. They're going to be taking them in this morning. There are just too many reporters out there!' Amelia explained.

Sophie was disappointed but understood why their mums would want to protect them. Yasmine was famous in her own right and Katie really wasn't one for cameras and fuss at the best of times.

After having some breakfast, a shower and a new school uniform out of the wardrobe, Sophie got the lift downstairs with her dad and the pair bravely ventured out to the car.

Reporters still lined up across the car park in front of Sophie's tower block. As soon as they saw Sophie coming towards them, they ran in her direction and started firing more questions at her and Tom. Sophie did her best to block them out and shut her eyes as she pushed away her dad's offer of help. All the unwanted attention on her made it almost impossible to get to the car. Eventually though, the pair made it; Tom had shouted down lots of reporters like yesterday and dismissed reports that Sophie was the first of a 'new wave' of mythical as utter nonsense.

Once inside the car, the reporters kept banging on the windows asking more and more questions. Dad had to take manual control of the car to avoid injuring anybody. He joked that he would love to run over a few feet like yesterday but his morals got the better of him.

While on the journey, Sophie looked out of the window and saw people going about their daily lives. Still, they were hypnotised by their screens and none of them were taking in the world around them. Sophie immediately felt sorry for them that, at the age of ten, she had just had a really exciting (if potentially dangerous) experience that most of them would never understand. She began to wonder how empty the lives of those people were and shook her head as she imagined that if the people just had a bit more imagination and drive, they could have something exciting happen to them.

Finally, and about half an hour late, Sophie arrived at school.

Chapter 8 – It Happened Again

It had been a hard slog for Sophie to get through to break time. She wanted so desperately to go through what had happened with her two best friends. Katie and Yasmine were also extremely close to Clara and Sophie knew that they missed her too. She had planned to talk to them before school but due to the reporters at home and then at school, Sophie was late. Mrs Tabard had grilled her and Tom when they had arrived, demanding an explanation for their lateness and saying the dinner ladies wouldn't be happy about having to add an extra meal to their already huge list of children they had to cook for.

During what was now her first maths lesson of the year, Sophie didn't dare do anything to attract Miss Sissins's attention – she just did her work and didn't even try to answer questions in front of the class like she usually did. Miss Sissins was being weird, glancing at Sophie occasionally when she thought she didn't notice and Sophie didn't like it. She was always eccentric and a bit over the top but the children adored her for it. She could make the most mundane thing exciting. However, this was different; yesterday she came across as nasty and frightening and Sophie thought it would be best to keep her head down. If it hadn't been for Miss Sissins doing break duty today, Sophie was certain she would try to keep her in so she could quiz her again. However, this meant that Sophie would get to have her chat, uninterrupted.

Eventually, after what felt like ice ages, break time arrived and Sophie whispered to Yasmine and Katie that they should meet up in the far corner of the field before everyone got their snack and darted outside. They were both sitting under the enormous willow tree in the corner, Yasmine wasn't looking at anything in particular and Katie was sitting with her hand on her cheek and elbow on her knee. The enormous weeping willow tree was always a great place to have a private conversation; it was the other end of the field to the school and all the reporters who were outside the grounds wouldn't be able to see over the fence and through the hedge onto the field. The school field was enormous and on either side of it were even more fields. Many the time the girls had joked that if the hedges separating the fields hadn't been there, they would have had the biggest school field in the world!

As Sophie drew closer, she could see that Yasmine was zoned out, surfing the net. This explained why Katie was showing no interest in talking to her.

'Are you sure it's sensible to be playing with that?' Sophie asked Yasmine, knowing full well she probably wasn't supposed to be using it at school.

'My dad has told me not to use it for now, so I haven't been at home, not like he can take it off me though is it?' Yasmine replied.

Sophie looked a bit worried by that rather flippant sentence but she let it go.

'Alton King hasn't been seen since yesterday,' Yasmine explained, 'says he arrived back at Shadow and hasn't been out of the building. There has been no comment about whether other children will get an implant anytime soon after your fainting.'

After that, Yasmine zoned back in again and looked at Sophie, who was blocking the sun out of Katie and Yasmine's eyes.

'All right, Katie?' Sophie asked her other friend.

Without making eye contact, Katie just shrugged and mumbled something about her mother that neither Yasmine nor Sophie, could make out. Sophie took that as if she was alright and sat down in between them on the grass.

'I need to tell you both something,' Sophie said in something ever so slightly louder than a whisper.

Katie stopped mumbling and seemed to snap out of her trance to turn and listen,

'Is it to do with yesterday?' she asked in a tone that was slightly louder than Sophie was comfortable with.

'Yes,' said Sophie, gesturing for Katie to turn her volume down; something she never thought she would have to worry about.

'Oh,' replied Katie.

'What's your problem?' Sophie asked, aggrieved.

'Nothing, it doesn't matter,' Katie replied, not being in the least bit convincing.

Something was bothering her but Sophie and Yasmine were both too preoccupied to notice properly let alone try to figure out what it was. If Katie wasn't just going to come out and say it then they weren't going to probe because Sophie had more important things to tell.

'Have either of you heard from Clara since she left?' Sophie asked.

The other two turned and looked at her. Over the six weeks holiday, the three of them had played together a lot and only at the start, when Clara had first left, did they talk about her. She had become a bit of a no-go area since she had gone – a friend who left without saying goodbye, in Katie's opinion especially, wasn't a friend at all. She had been abandoned before and didn't concern herself with anyone else that did it.

'You know we haven't,' Yasmine replied.

'Why would we want to see her anyway?' Katie added.

Sophie looked slightly annoyed at that comment. In spite of everything, Clara was the same age as them and would have no control over whether her dads wanted to leave. Sophie was sure that Clara would have said goodbye if she could, so to say something like that made Sophie a bit cross.

'She's my cousin,' Sophie said, aggrieved at Katie, 'and I saw her yesterday.'

'When?' Yasmine asked.

'When I passed out,' Sophie replied.

'You mean, like a dream?' Yasmine was trying to be sympathetic but was coming across as sarcastic.

Katie just rolled her eyes; the conversation had once again gone back to her so-called friend who had left them.

'No, it was more like a vision, like she was trying to communicate with me,' Sophie knew she sounded ridiculous and she was going to have a tough job convincing her friends.

Before Sophie could say anymore though, there was a deafening scream from the other side of the field and everyone stopped as it was so loud it could have been the whistle to signal the end of break.

It had come from a girl in year 2 named Rochelle, 'Reuben's fallen down,' she screeched.

Miss Sissins went running over and, sure enough, there was Reuben Houghton lying on the field. He was breathing but Miss Sissins shouted to Mrs Tabard – the other adult out on the field - 'He's fainted!'

Mrs Tabard asked calmly for one of the year sixes to go and tell the other teachers in the staffroom to send out another first aider to come and look at him with Mrs Tabard. Sure enough, Kieran Miller sprinted off.

Seeing all this from the other side of the field, Sophie started to feel a bit peculiar. She felt dizzy and like she was about to be sick. She turned to her left and saw that Yasmine was lying flat on the ground just like Reuben. Sophie's eyes went funny and her stomach turned. Before she could do anything else, Sophie was on the grass lying next to her.

It started much quicker this time. There were no lightning strikes or Sophie staring at nothingness. She just found herself, straight away looking at Clara's face. Clara looked even worse, this time she was lying down on what looked like an operating table and Sophie was looking at her as if she was standing next to her with Clara lying on her side. Also, around the table - like they were standing next to Sophie - were people in white coats, looking closely at Clara. If Sophie didn't know better she would have assumed they were doctors but it just had a much more dangerous vibe to it. Also, to the side of the white coats was a man with short brown hair and thin glasses wearing a black t-shirt and jeans. Clara was looking the wrong way to have seen him but he caught Sophie's attention briefly.

Then Clara began mouthing again and Sophie switched her gaze. Clara's eyes were black around the edges – she looked exhausted. Her cheeks were pale and her lips cracked. It didn't take Sophie long to see what she was mouthing this time. 'Get me out now!' Sophie said softly to herself. Relieved, Sophie then realised she didn't know how much time she had. She reached out to Clara and tried to touch her. Her hand went straight through Clara but her face changed to more of a calm look. Her petrified gaze had softened, almost as if she could sense the touch. Then, as Sophie stroked Clara's face, Clara changed again to red hair, then blonde, then brunette before back to Clara's regular black hair. It was like Sophie was looking at four or five different people, but the face eventually settled on the Clara whom Sophie knew.

'You can hear me!' Clara said out loud.

All the white coats heard her talk and stopped what they were doing to look at her. They said something to each other and started to panic but Sophie had no idea what they were saying or doing due to the surgical masks that covered their mouths. The bespectacled man in the corner was ushered out of the room despite his appeals.

'YES!' Sophie shouted back, but Clara didn't respond at all, she just looked around her, unable to locate Sophie's gaze. Sophie realised that she was invisible to her eyes but not to her touch. She reached over and let her hand roll over her face; knowing that if she applied pressure, her hand would just go through. Clara smiled a huge smile; the one that Sophie had grown up with before it flicked to four or five different faces again.

'Thank goodness for that!' Clara said out loud again and the frenzied actions of the white-coated people seemed to get even faster and more frantic.

All that passed Sophie by though because Clara looked happy. Sophie smiled and went to hold her cousin's hand; Clara went to squeeze the soft touch back but her hand went straight through Sophie's. Clara started to laugh through pained eyes.

'Thank you so much,' she said, fighting back tears.

Almost as soon as it had started, it finished and Sophie found herself back on the field. She was lying next to Yasmine who, along with Katie, was shaking her to try and wake her up – it had worked. Sophie sat herself up. She felt a bit hazy but ok nonetheless. The only thing that really bothered her was a red light that had appeared in the corner of her eye that kept flashing repeatedly. Sophie wiped her eye but the flashing persisted. Dismissing it as a side effect of fainting, Sophie focused on her friends again.

'It happened again, didn't it? I passed out again,' she asked, convinced she knew what the answer was going to be.

'No, *we* passed out,' Yasmine replied.

Sophie looked at Katie in shock; Katie just sat there nodding her head with her mouth open. Sophie was half right, it had happened again but not just to her this time! Across the field, Reuben Houghton was now sat up with Mrs Tabard giving him a drink of water, which one of the year fives had fetched. Worryingly, heading straight for Sophie was Miss Sissins and she didn't look friendly!

Kieran had raced off the field to find someone that could come and look at Reuben. He dashed up to the main entrance and banged on the door. He couldn't see anyone in the office to let him in, so he ran around to the back door of his classroom. He threw the door open and sprinted down the corridor. As he passed the door to Class 4 he caught sight of Miss Chorley, she was at her desk lying with her head on her arms.

'MISS!' he shouted; Miss Chorley didn't move. 'MISS!' he shouted a bit louder; still no response.

Kieran gave up and careered upstairs towards the staff room. He banged on the door but there was no answer. So, he banged again but still nothing. Having then waited for what felt like an age, Kieran turned the handle on the door.

Meanwhile, Miss Sissins continued her march over towards the three girls. She had fury in her eyes and her arms were waving about but not in the charismatic way they normally did. She was pointing and clenching her fists.

'WHAT DID SHE SAY?' she bellowed.

Sophie, Yasmine and Katie just stared at her, completely lost as to what to do. Sophie kept trying to shield herself from the flashing red light but couldn't. They had never seen their favourite teacher raise her voice at anyone, let alone three of the most trustworthy girls in school who hadn't actually done anything wrong.

'I KNOW YOU'VE SPOKEN TO CLARA, WHAT DID SHE SAY?'

By now Miss Sissins was only a few metres away from them and there looked to be no stopping her. The rest of the field was still in silence since the unusually loud scream indicated Reuben's faint. The only other noise was the gentle sway of the trees and Miss Sissins screaming. Even the cars outside on the roads seemed to have gone silent.

Miss Sissins arrived in front of them; she raised her index fingers on both hands and softened her voice slightly, 'Tell me what she said, I need to help her. You have no idea what you're dealing with; just tell me what you know.'

Sophie looked at her two friends; three days ago, she would have shared anything with Miss Sissins. She was always so kind and friendly. Now though she was genuinely terror-inducing. However, this time Sophie got the impression that she wasn't out to harm them. She seemed to be more desperate than angry now she could see her up close. She was just about in control of herself but she was incredibly lost in her own thoughts and clearly had an unbelievable amount of pressure on her. Sophie thought she looked frightened so she made the grown-up decision that it wouldn't do any harm to tell her, she was a woman in need of help, not being lied to. Bearing that in mind, Sophie decided to start talking.

'The first time I couldn't hear her,' Sophie said.

Miss Sissins breathed a huge sigh of relief and smiled.

'I had to make out what she was mouthing.'

'What are you doing?' Katie asked incredulously, still frightened at being shouted at.

'It's ok,' Sophie replied, not taking her gaze off Miss Sissins.

'What was she saying?' Miss Sissins asked.

'Get me…' Sophie began.

Just then a voice screamed from the other side of the field, 'MISS SISSINS, THEY'VE ALL FAINTED!' Kieran was standing at the entrance to the field and the whole school stopped looking at the argument at the other end of the field to hear the latest, exciting development.

Miss Sissins closed her eyes so as not to look at Sophie, Yasmine and Katie and shouted while turning around to face Kieran.

She started to walk forwards, knowing she was putting the well-being of everyone else before her own.

'They've what?' she asked.

'Unconscious or asleep or... something - every single one of them,' Kieran replied, racing across the field to meet Miss Sissins partway.

As Miss Sissins met him, Miss Chorley appeared at the entrance to the field. She looked extremely confused and could hardly stand up. Miss Sissins ran over to her. A few seconds later, Miss Chorley was sitting on the ground with a drink of water talking about how she had fallen asleep at her desk.

Eventually, all the other teachers and assistants made their way out onto the field. The classes lined up and went back in for their next lesson. Just a few minutes later, it would have been hard to tell that something had actually happened and this was most unusual to Sophie.

For the rest of the morning, Sophie couldn't shake the events of break time: Clara and what she might be going through, Miss Sissins seeming to be not the person everyone thought she was and all the teachers fainting. Something was weird, really weird. With all these new developments, Sophie had forgotten all about the reporters that were waiting for her outside of school. Although, oddly, as the clock ticked towards dinner time, Sophie took a trip to the toilet to examine the annoying red dot in her eye and, on the way, looked out the window that, due to the high point of the school, overlooked the road outside. They had all gone. Something hadn't just happened at Pinkleton Primary that break-time. There had been an event all over the world; the first such event since The Departure had caused the vanishing of the mythicals.

Chapter 9 – All Over the World

Over the course of the rest of the day, it became clear that all wasn't right outside school when Mrs Tabard kept coming to the classroom to ask for certain children to go home as their parents were there to collect them. None of them had any appointments and so the children that were left, which so far included Yasmine, Sophie and Katie, wondered what they were missing out on.

As she was banned from using her implant during lessons (it was seen to be an unfair advantage) Yasmine was unable to find out what was happening by looking on the internet. So, the three of them sat there being taught by Miss Sissins, who, having had it confirmed by Sophie that she had seen Clara, seemed to have got her head back together. The three of them wondered what on Earth was happening.

Just before dinner time, Mr Houghton, who had sent Reuben home straight after break, gathered the remaining handful of children in the hall and explained that schools up and down the country were closing and that their parents were coming to collect them all just as soon as they could get there. This really threw Sophie, Yasmine and Katie; this was starting to sound even more like one of her dad's stories about the olden days.

Eventually, Amelia arrived at school and explained to Mr Houghton that she was taking Yasmine home as well because her mum and dad were away with work and simply couldn't get back. Yasmine and Sophie gathered their things together and waved goodbye to Katie, who was now stuck at school pretty much by herself with just Mr Houghton and a few infants to talk to.

'Lucky Katie,' Yasmine remarked sarcastically as she got up to leave.

'Your mum is coming to get you as soon as she can, Katie,' Amelia said to her as she led Sophie and Yasmine away.

Katie just grunted and half-waved; she was feeling left out and annoyed that Clara was being mentioned again, now she was being abandoned at school as well, she really wanted to talk to her friends and have them take an interest in her and her problem but they didn't seem at all bothered.

When the three had climbed into the car and once Amelia had input the destination, Sophie, who was still seeing a red flashing light in the corner of her eye, was quizzed by Yasmine. Yasmine considered using her implant but thought it would be polite and more sociable to talk in person. Both Sophie and Yasmine listened to what Amelia had to say and soon became horrified at what they heard.

Amelia explained that at 10:19 all over the world people just stopped whatever they were doing and passed out. Sophie and Yasmine looked at each other.

'That was the time when...' Yasmine started but Sophie interrupted.

'Yes, that was the time when *you* fainted,' Sophie stared at Yasmine and with the two being such good friends, Yasmine knew exactly what Sophie was saying without actually saying anything – don't tell my mum!

'You fainted as well Yasmine!' Amelia shrieked.

'Yes, so did Reuben Houghton,' Yasmine added.

'Dear me, there are things on the news – builders falling off scaffolding, people nearly drowning in swimming pools, babies being left unsupervised. Fortunately, they're saying it only lasted for about 60 seconds and with self-driving cars and planes it would have been much worse a few years ago – people falling asleep at the wheel and what have you,' Amelia came up for air. 'Ignore whatever your dad says; he insists it's telekinetic parasites taking over everyone's mind or two parallel worlds colliding. Take it from me though, the mythicals are not returning.'

Normally Sophie would have smiled at this comment, imagining her dad rummaging through all his old books, newspaper cuttings and conspiracy websites, trying to prove that the olden days had returned. However, after the events of today, Sophie was beginning to think that there might be some truth in it. The mythicals hadn't been seen in any capacity for ten years, nothing exciting or unusual had happened on Earth since The Departure, outside of Shadow releasing more and more mind-zapping gadgets. Sophie was starting to put some pieces together, she didn't know if they were correct but all this definitely sounded like the start of one of her dad's stories from years gone by.

'Was it just you and Reuben that passed out Yazz or did anyone else?' Amelia asked, still showing the concern you would expect of a mother.

'No, no one else. Kieran ran to the staffroom because Miss Sissins told him to after Reuben fainted and he said that all the teachers had,' Sophie added.

'But Miss Sissins didn't?' Amelia noticed.

Yasmine and Sophie looked at each other. Having only just heard the story of what had happened everywhere, the two had failed to put together the fact that all the adults fainted except for Miss Sissins and, for that matter, Mrs Tabard. Why hadn't they passed out?

'Well with Reuben and Yasmine both fainting it must be to do with the implants. Does that mean Miss Sissins doesn't have one?' Amelia added.

'Clearly not' Sophie said intrigued, she racked her brains but couldn't remember seeing her with one.

'But she's young, likes her technology; she's a wiz with that whiteboard in your classroom,' Amelia continued.

Sophie and Yasmine were getting more intrigued. It was understandable why Mrs Tabard didn't need access to the internet – she was much more old-fashioned than most people and still did everything with pen and paper, but Miss Sissins? This didn't make sense.

Yasmine zoned out and started accessing the implant to read the news reports. Amelia turned hers on to send Tom a message saying that they were all ok and on the way home. Sophie was left to ponder what was going on but most of all one question, which seemed to have escaped Yasmine - if it was all because of the implants, which it seemed to clearly be, why had Sophie passed out as well? She had fainted on the stage before the implant had been successful she thought. The red light continued to flash and it was starting to irritate Sophie.

By the time the car had arrived home and Sophie, her mum and Yasmine had gotten up to their flat, the rest of the world seemed to have fathomed the connection between the Internet Implants and the blackouts. Reporters, who were previously haunting Sophie, were now lining the steps up to the Shadow HQ waiting for an interview with Alton King. Sophie wondered why more didn't want to interview the 'Singularity' (the nickname that she had first heard Mr Houghton use was growing on her) as she was, strictly speaking, the first to faint – albeit yesterday. Maybe the reporters wanted King first as he could provide actual answers, whereas Sophie could only speculate. The reporters also had no idea that Sophie had fainted again today, even her own mum didn't know that! Sophie and Yasmine sat on the settee, learning as much as they could but pondering about what to do next.

Through the news reports, Sophie noticed that the olden days were being mentioned again for the first time in years. Normally, the news never referred to them anymore, they just glossed over them like they never happened along with the rest of society. Now, however, the presenters were showing images of similar mass 'faintings' that had happened throughout history. There was nothing even vaguely on the same scale as what the world had experienced today. Three hundred people at once in Trafalgar Square about a century ago, five hundred people at a football match sixty-six years ago. Today's event had been more like five billion, not five hundred!

When dad arrived home, he told Sophie and Yasmine all the possibilities he could think of. He sat them down at the dinner table with huge scrapbooks of cuttings and writings that he had collected over the years.

'This is everything I have,' he started, 'every clue to every event that ever took place that I could get my hands on,' he was talking with the same passion that he showed when he told Sophie stories – it was because of this enthusiasm that Sophie had struck up an interest in it in the first place, now Yasmine was listening intently too.

'From everything I have ever read, every website I have ever been on, every person I have ever spoken to, I have come up with the following conclusions,' he sat forward and flicked through the first of the scrapbooks.

Newspaper clippings fell out, photos of goodness knows what and scribblings in writings that Sophie had no clue what they said as she didn't even recognise the letters.

'Here we are – first of all, I think there was a secret group of people somewhere who stepped in, in secret, when there was an incident with a mythical. Every single event just seemed to stop. Take for example the Draining of Venice, I know I've told you about that one before, one minute the water was gone and everyone was panicking as that alien – can't remember its name now – threatened to completely drain the planet, what was its name? Next minute, Venice has flooded again and the alien has vanished,' Tom came up for breath, but then quickly started again, 'are you telling me that that situation just sorted itself out?'

'No dad,' Sophie said, 'you think some band of people secretly stopped him.'

Tom said nothing but Sophie could see the glint in his eye at that last comment. Then, when that moment had passed, he started up again.

'Where did that alien go? I hear you ask…well, based on these photos here…' Tom slid some pictures of the countryside under Sophie and Yasmine's noses, which to Sophie and Yasmine looked simply like photos of the countryside. There were three houses all in a row which had steps up to them. One had a green door but to Sophie and everyone else they just looked like houses in the middle of nowhere, '… and these records here,' he then slid a piece of paper that had been horribly smudged on top of the photos, 'I think that this secret society of people locks all these creatures in a place called…Sadcore or Melonoria. There seem to be two separate places, I can't fathom which!'

Even Sophie, who normally loved her dad's stories couldn't contain a laugh, Yasmine was practically on the floor; Tom had gone too far.

'So, you're telling us that there are secret agents all over the world locking up all the mythicals from the olden days in a prison called "Sadcore" or a place called Melonoria?'

'Yes,' Tom replied 'it's in the countryside somewhere.'

'I'm going to watch TV,' Yasmine said.

'No, stay,' Sophie insisted.

Yasmine reluctantly listened more as Tom reeled off more things he had uncovered. None of it related in any way to the blackout today but it was one of her dad's stories and Sophie listened even more than usual as this one was putting today into context – Sophie was loving it even more than usual because she was living this story of her very own!

Chapter 10 – Releasing a Statement

Sat round in his office, Alton King had reached the end of his tether. The room contained nothing except a desk and chair. The desk had one fat, black leg at the front which arched inwards and the top was glass, on top that there was nothing. King was sat deep in thought, but not the sort of thought that inspired him to create or invent, he was stressed and if he wasn't careful, the next thing he said to the press could ruin him and the company that he had worked from scratch to build up. And that to him would be worse than the end of the world!

It was clear to him as well now that the implant, which had been invented by a small group of very clever scientists in that very office right there in Shadow HQ, was the main factor in all its users fainting at once, but if he told the press this it would cause mass panic. Everyone had one – rich, poor, famous, insignificant, almost every person in the developed world had one. They had become part of everyday life and people relied on them for everything including news – you could be placed in augmented reality and stand face-to-face with a news reporter on the scene. Films – you were now totally immersed in a film, it was like having a 360-degree view of everything going on around you. Something as simple as selecting music to listen to or changing television channels was now all done in mind, bus travel and even toilet visits were now dominated by people using their implants. People were never bored, they were totally immersed. It was about as far away from the olden days of terrifying creatures as you could get and Alton King had made that happen!

When the blackout occurred, he had been studying lines of code in the system from the moment when Sophie fainted the first time, just trying to see what had happened. When the second, infinitely larger, fainting had taken place, King had been sat at his desk looking at a real-time feed of what was happening underneath the surface of the implant's huge storage database, which was stored at its facility – Stratus - examining code.

Stratus tower had been built in the centre of London and was home to everything that the internet needed to function – the hub that emitted the signal for everyone to use and feed off in their quest to stay online, its signal and the servers. The Shadow HQ however was King's normal base of operations and main 'home' to everything internet related but it was Stratus that served as the beating heart of the internet experience and would act as a backup if anything was ever to go wrong at Shadow HQ.

King too had passed out and when he awoke 60 seconds later, he noticed something within the code – lines of numbers that shouldn't have been there. They were words written in old binary, where letters were replaced by numbers.

01000111 01100101 01110100 00100000 01101101 01100101 00100000 01101111 01110101 01110100 00101100 00100000 01101110 01101111 01110111 00100001

He had studied them carefully for a minute and translated them – 'Get me out, now!' read the message.

King instantly knew who it was and exactly who to get in contact with to help, it then occurred to him that although he knew who he needed, he had no way of getting in touch with them as that person never opened their messages. One thing he definitely knew for sure and could deal with now was he had to delete the code before anyone else saw it. He did so without giving it a second thought. This was the decision he was faced with – keep quiet and hope everything went away or tell someone and risk losing everything. The world saw him as a genius and a visionary; he didn't want that to change. He *was* a genius, he *was* a visionary. He had changed the world and he didn't want that taken away from him. His company was his livelihood and everything he had – this wasn't a decision to be taken lightly.

He was given ten minutes of thinking time before his alert flashed on his implant. Outside the offices were some reporters (there hadn't been any around him for years). They tended to leave him well alone as they knew he was responsible for all the advancement of the human race and he never seemed to leave his offices so he couldn't be doing anything exciting or worthy of reporting on. The message said that they wanted to know if he had anything to add to the quickly spreading rumour that all implant users had fainted at the same time and that a fault in the Internet Implant or the hub in Stratus was to blame. He had never faced a crisis like this before. He wasn't sure what to do.

He ignored the alert about the reporters and in the meantime more and more arrived.

Half an hour later, and with the press now really hankering after the interview that they were promised twenty minutes ago, he had a plan – lie! *The code doesn't exist anymore,* he thought to himself. *Why should anyone know any different? This invention is too important to mankind now to throw it all away because of one glitch!*

After convincing himself he was doing the right thing, he opened his office door and walked towards the main entrance where the press was waiting outside at the bottom of the steps. With some notes in his hand, he stood at the top of the stairs, shuffled his papers and started telling the world it wasn't down to him or his invention.

Sat at home, Sophie and Yasmine watched King on the news, still pondering over Tom's efforts to convince them he knew what was going on. Throughout the whole shambles, they knew he was lying. Three people had fainted on that school field and all three had had something to do with an implant just the day before. Sophie's mind was going into overdrive.

'He's lying,' she said, rubbing her eye.

'How do you know?' Amelia's voice came from the kitchen.

'Err, just a feeling,' Sophie mumbled, not realising that her mum could hear her.

'Yes, he is,' Yasmine added, 'what are you doing with your face?' she asked, noticing Sophie was still rubbing her eye.

'Nothing, I'm fine,' Sophie lied.

'But what do we do about it?' Yasmine asked, 'There's only us two; unless you count Miss Sissins and I don't trust her right now.'

'I'm not sure that she can't be trusted either. Maybe we talk to her if we can't think of anyone else,' Sophie replied, 'What about Reuben? We don't know what he saw, or if he saw anything at all.'

A thought struck Yasmine, 'What about Mr Houghton, if it wasn't for him, we wouldn't be here. He put us in that competition, he picked out the children. Why pick you and me? Two girls from year 6 in the first three people, that doesn't seem right. You'd think it would be more spread across school.'

'We need to ask him for more information about this competition he entered us in,' Sophie agreed, 'we can ask him tomorrow.'

Yasmine sat back and folded her arms with a rather smug look on her face, 'This is like being a detective,' she said, excitedly.

'Yes, but, there's one really big question that you still haven't asked me yet,' Sophie said, waiting for Yasmine to realise that she had fainted apparently without having an implant inside her.

Yasmine stared at her completely baffled. After a few minutes of Sophie tormenting Yasmine that she wasn't as good a detective as she made out (as detectives wouldn't miss the big questions), Sophie caved in and told her. Yasmine looked puzzled.

After a few seconds of silence, Sophie also told her about Clara's second appearance. Yasmine said that she remembered nothing but blackness when she passed out. Clara wanted to talk to Sophie and nobody else, or so Sophie thought.

Chapter 11 – A Brief Moment of Calm

By the next morning, parents had discussed what they thought should happen via various chat groups and other social media and agreed that their children would be better off carrying on as normal. Katie's mum had said Katie had spent all afternoon talking with Mr Houghton as she just couldn't get off work to go and fetch her. Letting them stay at home all day to watch TV would just scare them and, if another blackout was to occur, the children would probably be much safer at school than at home or wandering the streets. As a result, Sophie and Yasmine (who had stayed over at Sophie's that night) walked to school the day after.

Yasmine started straightening Sophie's spare school jumper that she had borrowed, 'I've been thinking,' she said.

'Were you sitting down at the time, you know it's dangerous when you do that standing up?' Sophie asked with jovial undertones.

Yasmine simply tilted her head in acknowledgement of the mickey taking and carried on talking,'

'If you get to be called Singularity because of the incident the day before yesterday...'

Was it only that long ago? Sophie thought to herself, so much had happened in less than 48 hours.

'Then I should get a nickname as well, we're about to do all this spying and crime-fighting together and I was the first child to get an implant I'm probably more important than you!'

Yasmine meant no harm by this. It may have sounded rude but Sophie knew her friend well enough to know she didn't mean it like that.

'OK, what were you thinking?' Sophie asked cautiously. At this point, Sophie noticed some people on the other side of the street, whispering and pointing in their direction. Fame was clearly beginning to set in for her and Yasmine. The pair waved and carried on walking.

Yasmine reached around and unzipped her bag. Out of it, she took the thesaurus that lived on Tom's bookshelf. Sophie asked her mum once why she still had one when nowadays all books were read online. She had told her that dad always said it was good to have books in the house because they couldn't be tampered with or changed like things online could be.

'What are you doing with that?' Sophie asked, perplexed that Yasmine felt so comfortable in Sophie's house that she would just take something without asking.

'It's helping me find a better word for 'First' as I was the first child with an implant my name should reflect that!' Yasmine replied, completely oblivious to Sophie's perplexity.

'Oh well in that case...' Sophie began but was cut off before she could finish.

'Here we are, foremost...'

'No.'

'...Principal...'

'No'

'...Paramount...'

'Best so far'

'...Uppermost...'

'Go with Paramount'

'NO! Here it is! Singularity, I'd like you to meet your new partner… Prime,' Yasmine stood with her hands on her hips doing her best superhero pose, which looked kind of silly in a lilac school uniform.

Sophie smiled at her friend, 'OK 'Prime', I accept. Together we shall investigate a huge company that is responsible for the mass fainting of billions of people around the world and prove that they are lying… even though we're only 10 years old.'

'How exactly are we going to do that?' Yasmine asked, 'What do we do first?'

'We're going to talk to Mr Houghton about the competition and see how exactly we won and what he had to do. Why we haven't heard which other schools entered? Why was it so important that he moved his own son here? We have a lot to ask him!' Sophie had written this plan down and a host of questions on a piece of paper.

'Why didn't you use an online thesaurus just then?' Sophie asked, realising that her best friend had missed an opportunity to use her new implant.

'And miss talking to you! This is much better, spies don't communicate through the internet. That would leave a trail that any government hacks could follow!' Yasmine really had learnt all the spy 'lingo'.

Sophie smiled at her best friend as she seemed to be enjoying all this despite everyone all over the world fainting!

'Pooh, this is so electrifying, adrenaline-charged and exhilarating,' Yasmine was nearly bursting!

'Put the thesaurus away!' Sophie tutted and smiled then rubbed her eye again. The flashing was really annoying her now. She thought it might have disappeared after a night's sleep but apparently not.

This was it, they were going for it. Unbeknown to them, about fifty paces behind them down the road, Katie was walking to school by herself with her shoulders hunched and hood up.

Sophie's original plan was to arrive at school early and go straight to Mr Houghton's office. This didn't work though because he hadn't arrived yet and Mrs Tabard, who was running breakfast club that morning, said that he had dropped Reuben off there (and would be for the next few days while he got some stuff sorted) and said that he would be in slightly later as he had an important meeting, nothing unusual for a head teacher. Sophie and Yasmine stood around on the playground waiting for the whistle to go so that they could line up. There were no reporters there at all this morning; they had all got bigger stories about potential new mythicals coming to invade Earth by making everyone faint. Nobody was particularly bothered about one 10-year-old girl anymore, apart from some of the younger girls in years 2 and 3 who seemed to be looking up to Sophie and copying some of the things she did (like the way she stood or they now had the same bag or coat as her). While they were waiting, Katie came up to Sophie and Yasmine.

'Hey,' she muttered quietly.

'Hello, what happened to you yesterday?' Sophie asked.

'I was stuck at school until my mum could get off work,' Katie replied, 'Mr Houghton was telling me something interesting about...' Katie paused, 'It wouldn't matter to you,' Katie desperately wanted her two friends to ask her to finish the story but neither of them seemed to be listening, so she changed the topic.

'What have you been up to?' Katie asked.

'Oh, we just came up with a plan to...' Yasmine also only got part way through her sentence before Sophie cut her off.

'Stop!' Sophie shouted, then realised she had shouted and looked round to see who was listening. There were some children from lower down the school looking in her direction but Sophie assumed that they were still interested in Singularity as they were too young to understand the blackout.

Katie look baffled, she still wanted the two of them to ask her about yesterday but they weren't bothered or hadn't noticed. As a result, she gestured for Sophie to offer an explanation as to why she had just shouted so loudly.

'We're really sorry but we can't tell you,' Sophie said, apologetically.

'Fine,' said Katie, 'not like we tell each other stuff anymore.'

Yasmine stepped in to try and offer an explanation and to calm her friend down, 'It's been a busy two days!'

'Yes, but you could let me know what's happening, couldn't you?' Katie never raised her voice, this was the angriest Sophie and Yasmine had seen her.

'We'll tell you everything when we get the chance,' Sophie explained.

'Whatever,' Katie said and she stormed off to a different part of the playground.

Before she was out of earshot, Yasmine asked, 'What's her problem?'

'We've got quite a lot going on and there is a lot she doesn't know,' Sophie began, 'we're supposed to be best friends. We need to tell her things or she'll just stop talking to us.'

Before Yasmine could reply, the whistle went and everyone joined their class lines. Miss Sissins came out with a bit more of a smile on her face than yesterday and lead the class in.

Chapter 12 – Trying to tackle it 'Head' on

Maths had never felt so long! Having found out that Mr Houghton wouldn't be in until later, Sophie and Yasmine agreed, quietly, that their next best chance to go and talk to him would be at break time. From 9:00 until 10:15, the girls would have to make do with place value of decimals up to three places. They could both do it standing on their heads but they needed to prove that they understood it, what with them doing tests at the end of the year. Every now and then Sophie would think of something else that they needed to ask Mr Houghton and made a quick note on a well-hidden piece of paper. Occasionally, Miss Sissins would come around to their table and look at how Yasmine and Sophie were doing. Sophie no longer thought she would launch into more questions about Clara and Sophie's vision; she was now acting as if nothing had happened.

About two minutes before break time, Mrs Tabard appeared in the classroom and Ryan tutted and got up to head for his bag because he guessed he had forgotten his dinner money *again*!

'Sit down Ryan; it isn't you that I want this time,' Mrs Tabard said, beleaguered, 'Although if you do want to pay me for next week's meals you can do!'

Ryan slumped back down and rolled his eyes. Normally, Miss Sissins would have dealt with this but she seemed somewhat distracted by Mrs Tabard's arrival. Mrs Tabard looked at Miss Sissins and mimed 'a phone call in the office' by putting her hand next to her head and stretching out her thumb and little finger. Sophie questioned the point in miming this as she may as well have just said it; all the children had worked out the mime anyway. Then Sophie's thought changed – everyone knew that school had a phone in case of emergencies, such as the one yesterday but why was someone ringing Miss Sissins? This was yet more evidence that she didn't have an implant, but why and who was it? Sophie had never heard Miss Sissins talk about a family of her own. She was very quickly distracted though as Miss Sissins checked the time and dismissed the class early for break and they all hurriedly rushed outside. Katie hung around, hoping that Sophie or Yasmine would come and start a conversation with her but they got their snack ready as quickly as possible and headed straight for Mr Houghton's office, oblivious to Katie, who took herself outside.

On their way there, they overtook Mrs Tabard, who was still making her way back to the office. Mrs Tabard took exception to the speed at which they had 'walked' down the corridor.

'Are you two supposed to be inside at break?' she asked, making herself sound important.

'Err, yes,' Yasmine stuttered, 'we're on our way to Mr Houghton's office,' Yasmine had always been good at bending the truth slightly or exaggerating. It all added to her drama queen persona.

'Nothing serious I hope,' said Mrs Tabard, sounding disappointed in the pair of them despite the fact that neither of them had actually done anything wrong, other than walk up the corridor a bit quickly!

'No, we just wanted to talk to someone about the last few days,' Yasmine said, 'Sophie is still in a bit of shock.'

At this, Sophie started to pretend to cry. It was so convincing that Mrs Tabard sent them on their way immediately. She didn't do tears or sympathy very well and she carried on her own journey back to the office.

When Yasmine and Sophie arrived at Mr Houghton's office, they knocked gently.

'Come in,' chimed Mr Houghton.

Sophie entered first, followed by Yasmine and the pair waited to be asked to sit down – as was the custom in the head teacher's office. Mr Houghton was making notes on a piece of paper and smiling as he did so.

'Sit down girls, is everything ok?' he asked, conscientiously.

'No, not really,' Sophie began.

She was feeling incredibly nervous. She had spoken to Mr Houghton a million times before but this was different. She had never been on the hunt for vital information from him before. He had always been such a kind man, a little over the top with enthusiasm but she had never been afraid of him. His huge, lumbering frame towered over the pair of them even though he was sitting down, making them feel even smaller.

'Oh dear, is it the last two days? Has it all been a bit much?' he asked.

'Yes and no,' Yasmine interjected, 'we were just wondering, to start with, with everything that is going on, why you picked us two to have the implant put in?'

Sophie scowled at her friend. Yasmine wasn't exactly going for discreet or subtle ways of asking questions, she was launching feet first into the *key* questions. Sophie hoped against hope that Mr Houghton wouldn't get suspicious. She need not have worried; Mr Houghton rocked back on his chair and smiled.

'My dears, I have faith in every child in this school. I could have picked any of you. Yasmine, you stood out because of your confidence and brashness. You can do anything you want in your life and I know that an implant would help you immensely. Also, you are the sort of person who wouldn't be fazed by being the first child to get one, you would just shrug off any attention you didn't like and it wouldn't bother you. You were born to be on camera and in the limelight, earning all the praise that goes with it. I have a lot of admiration for that.'

Yasmine beamed from ear to ear. That was one of the most wonderful things anyone had ever said to her. It was certainly unexpected from Mr Houghton who, quite often, struggled to remember some of the children's names. It was more the sort of thing that Miss Sissins would have said.

'What about me?' Sophie then asked, hoping for a similar answer and also doing away with the softly, softly approach to the questioning.

The smile remained on Mr Houghton's face, 'Sophie Hardy – you work so hard, you have so little. You are, my dear, one of the brightest minds I have ever seen and worked with and I have been working with children for *thousands* of years,' Mr Houghton smiled at his own hyperbole, 'If anyone can do amazing things with access to a whole universe of information – it's you. Your potential is limitless. Also, you are proving that being famous and receiving attention are positive things and that you deserve all the good things that are going to come soon. Your desire for betterment is completely unique on this planet.'

The compliments had thrown the girls. They had come into the office expecting Mr Houghton to be hard to read and hard to get information out of. He was quite the opposite; he was talking freely and openly. Sophie and Yasmine relaxed in their seats and as a result, their questions got even more relaxed, straight to the point and chatty – not the kind of conversation you would have with a head teacher.

'Why did you pick Reuben?' Yasmine asked.

Mr Houghton shuffled in his seat at this question, 'He's my son; I want the best for him. He too would have no problem handling the limelight of fame.' His answer was short and sharp, nothing like the other answers he had given so far.

Yasmine hadn't noticed the shortness, whereas Sophie had. Sophie wasn't going to continue asking about Reuben, but Yasmine ploughed on, 'Don't you think it's a bit unfair on the other children at school? He wasn't one of us until this week.'

She had gone too far. Mr Houghton rubbed his chin and wasn't smiling or acting relaxed anymore. He looked flustered and a bit cross that one of the children in his school would accuse him of being unfair. He had spent years priding himself on fairness at Pinkleton and here he was being questioned on it. Eventually, he just smiled and gave a short 'ha!' at the girls as if he had answered their question.

'Is there anything else?' Mr Houghton asked.

Yasmine turned to Sophie; she didn't understand why Mr Houghton hadn't answered her question. Sophie did and signalled for Yasmine to stop and move on or risk their cover being blown.

'Yes, the competition,' Sophie began, effortlessly changing the subject, 'can you tell us about it?'

'Not really,' Mr Houghton's shortness was decidedly noticeable now and Sophie didn't know how to make him relax again. However, she could understand why Reuben was a touchy subject, but the competition? Surely, he had nothing to hide there.

'What did you have to do? Why did we win? How many other schools entered?' Yasmine was getting frustrated at Mr Houghton's lack of compliance. She had forgotten where she was and what the relationship between pupil and head teacher should be.

Sophie glared at her again, but before she could say anything, Mr Houghton raised his voice.

'Look, I know what you're doing and I know what you want,' he was bordering on angry now; he snapped in such a way that Yasmine instantly stopped talking and realised that she had stepped over the line!

Sophie took a deep breath as she thought the two of them had pushed it too far and that Mr Houghton was going to send them outside and their quest would be over.

'You want to know who the other two were going to be, don't you?' Mr Houghton said and Sophie breathed out, 'Yes, we had to stop after Sophie fainted, which meant only three of the five children were implanted and you want to know who was going to be next.'

Sophie afforded herself a brief smile of relief; they had gotten away with it.

'You think if you can gather all the information that you can work it out. I have to say girls, some people have flat-out asked me, parents have threatened me, bribed me and I haven't told anyone. This is the first time someone has tried to quiz me and piece together clues to work it out. It reminds me of the time…' Mr Houghton was blabbering now like he did to parents.

Sophie shrugged at Yasmine; that was the signal to wrap up and quit while they were ahead. 'Yes, that's it,' Yasmine interrupted, now wanting to get out of the office before Mr Houghton launched into one of his long stories.

'OK, you got us,' Sophie said putting her hands up and going to stand up to make it clear to Mr Houghton that they wanted to leave.

He noticed that the girls had had enough and so decided not to tell his long-winded story, 'Well tried girls, you got a lot closer than some of the adults, but I'm afraid I just can't tell you!'

Sophie and Yasmine both stood up and headed towards the exit.

'Have you heard from Clara since she moved Sophie?' Mr Houghton asked.

Without thinking, Sophie replied 'Yes, I spoke to her yester…day.'

Sophie turned back and looked at Mr Houghton, instantly regretting what she had just said. Mr Houghton looked like a different person. The mild-manned head teacher had gone. The person sitting in his chair was still the same man as before but he looked decidedly more evil. His eyes pierced Sophie and his hands were clasped with his elbows on the arms of his chair, he smiled a vicious grin. He had clearly realised what they had come to him for and he had played them at their own game and broken them with one question whereas Sophie and Yasmine had come away with relatively nothing from all their long-planned efforts.

Before Sophie had a chance to think or react, or Mr Houghton had the opportunity to ask any more questions, there was a knock on the office door and it flung open before Mr Houghton could say 'come in'.

'Girls, a word, please. Now!' said Miss Sissins sounding urgent.

Chapter 13 – Trust Me

Miss Sissins almost pulled Yasmine and Sophie out of the office. She pointed in the direction of the classroom and indicated for the girls to walk. The girls didn't look at each other, just straight ahead. Surely the truth about Clara and the visions was about to come out to her parents, now that Mr Houghton knew Sophie had contacted her. Sophie imagined him being on a call with them right now telling them. Yasmine opened the door to the classroom and marched in. Both the girls turned very slowly to face Miss Sissins. They were frightened and just stood there, silent.

Miss Sissins launched into a hurricane of words and flying arms, 'What on Earth are you playing at? Going around calling each other Prime and Singularity – that isn't how all this works! Playing detectives with adults at 10 years old, interrogating one of the world's most dangerous men on your own with no training! I don't even know where to start!'

It was the bit about interrogating a dangerous man that made Yasmine break out of her reverie of nerves, 'Pardon!' she interrupted.

Miss Sissins paused and looked most put out that she had been cut off mid-flow and twisted her head to look at Yasmine in particular, her arms stopped flailing about and she simply looked at her like she had asked the most ridiculous, obvious question ever. She raised one eyebrow, 'Yes, one of the most dangerous men on Earth, well, I say Earth, any of the known planets really.' Miss Sissins lost her gaze on Yasmine, curled up her nose and started looking at the ceiling. She had distracted herself by trying to correct what she had said as if it made any difference to Sophie and Yasmine.

Yasmine stopped her before she started distracting herself even more, 'You're telling us that our head teacher is dangerous!' Yasmine said this like she couldn't (understandably) believe what she was hearing.

'Yes,' said Miss Sissins, arriving back from where ever it was her mind had just taken her, 'very.'

Yasmine snorted with impromptu laughter. Mr Houghton had been at school for years. They had both known him since they were about 6; he refused to bring hot drinks into the classroom in case of an accident because he was so safety conscious. He once saw a dog on the field, ran outside, caught it, advertised for its owners to come and find it, didn't find any and so adopted the dog himself! He was a bit over the top sometimes, he tended to bore people with his lectures (or as he called them 'stories') but he wasn't evil or dangerous, not to Yasmine at least.

'What's he done?' Yasmine asked, having now gotten over the snorts.

'He's lied to and manipulated many people, he's unnecessarily put the whole planet in mortal danger just to satisfy himself, he is cold, calculated and would throw his own family into a fire if it meant he could get what he wanted,' Miss Sissins listed then paused.

'He's our head teacher; he can't have done those things,' Yasmine said, not believing a word of it.

Sophie on the other hand was thinking back to the last few seconds before Miss Sissins pulled them out of his office. Something about Mr Houghton's face when he heard what Sophie said about

Clara meant she was giving this a lot more consideration than Yasmine was.

'…he also arranged the kidnap and disappearance of your cousin and her parents,' Miss Sissins concluded.

Something in Sophie snapped at hearing this; this final revelation was the one that made it for her. Just a few minutes earlier she would have laughed this off as one of Miss Sissins's jokes (albeit a very distasteful one) but now, having seen Mr Houghton the way he was as she left the office and seeing Miss Sissins now with her dead straight face, she knew it was true and wanted answers. Sophie immediately turned to leave through the door; she needed space to think and process the last few minutes. Miss Sissins blocked her exit so Sophie turned back on herself and Miss Sissins had to run around to block her exit from the back door.

'I need a minute!' Sophie screamed at Miss Sissins, Yasmine stood and watched on, helpless.

'I know you do Soph, but you can't go out there,' Miss Sissins said calmly, 'I am deadly serious about this, just sit down and hear me out. There are only two minutes of break left. I can give you the basics.'

Trying really hard to keep her emotions in check, Sophie looked at Miss Sissins. She could see a soft dread yet cold warmth in her eyes. It became even more obvious that she wasn't lying. She had spent a year in her class and knew when she was telling the truth and when she was having somebody on; this was no joke.

'OK,' Sophie said, pulling out her chair and sitting down at her table.

'What!' shrieked Yasmine, not quite believing what her friend had just said.

'We came to school today to find answers,' Sophie explained to Yasmine, 'we weren't going to get anything else out of Mr Houghton; he went a bit weird and then, when he asked about Clara…'

Sophie paused and couldn't begin to explain herself to Yasmine without sounding ridiculous so changed what she was going to say. She would never believe from one glance that Sophie saw that Mr Houghton wasn't who they had assumed, 'This is our best chance now.'

'I just need two minutes Yazz, trust me' said Miss Sissins, turning her gaze towards her.

Yasmine tutted, rolled her eyes and muttered to herself about how stupid this was before eventually she sat down next to Sophie and Miss Sissins sat at a chair at right angles to them. It wasn't the source they started out hoping to get their answers from, they didn't even know if they were going to be the answers that they wanted but they were going to get some now, like them or not!

Chapter 14 – Origins

'I work for an agency that monitors and defeats all the different evils that threaten the safety and wellbeing of the people on this planet,' Miss Sissins immediately blurted out.

Yasmine stared at her blankly as she clearly didn't believe any of it; Sophie on the other hand thought back to what her dad had told her last night about a group of people protecting the Earth.

'We have been around for many, many decades, we were the reason the mythicals never won and I am personally responsible for them disappearing.'

Sophie and Yasmine's looks didn't change. Miss Sissins carried on regardless, 'I am not a primary school teacher by trade; I was assigned here to primarily keep an eye on, as you know him, Mr Houghton.'

'Break time is nearly over,' Yasmine said like she was bored and had had enough.

Miss Sissins ignored her and got more animated, 'You have read in your books, and learnt from your dad, Sophie, that for years, Earth was subject to horrible, torturous events. How do you think these were stopped?'

Yasmine pondered, Sophie on the other hand just said, 'You?'

'That's right,' Miss Sissins started again, 'our agents worked tirelessly and secretly to keep everyone safe. We operated completely covertly and never came out of the shadows.'

Sophie put two and two together and got four straight away, 'Shadow?'

It was at this point that, along with Sophie, Yasmine now found herself starting to believe Miss Sissins, remembering the small amount she had heard Tom say the night before. She leant forward on the table, wanting to hear more.

'Before they were a technology company, Shadow operated as the agency that helped defeat the mythicals. When The Departure happened, it started to use the technology it had to make the human race better. Mr King has been at the forefront of that for ten years now and Mr Houghton and I are the only other ones left,' Miss Sissins continued.

'So, why is Mr Houghton so dangerous and you aren't?' Sophie asked.

'He started out as one of the founding members but he had a very different idea compared to others of where the agency should go next.'

'Which was?' Sophie asked.

'He wanted the public to be told about all our secrets and agents so that they could treat them as superheroes and worship them, thanking them for keeping the human race out of the darkness. In a way, I can completely see why he wanted it. We had people putting their necks on the line in gravely dangerous situations and regular people didn't even know it! Why shouldn't we get a pat on the back?'

'What did he do?' Sophie asked.

'He started rallying together all the agents, getting them to see things from his point of view, promising them ever-lasting fame and fortune. They instantly and understandably agreed. They wanted the publicity and to be adored; what they were doing was incredibly dangerous, and of course, they thought they should be rewarded.

Before long he had most of the workforce championing him and demanding to go public so that the agents of Shadow would become famous the world over.'

'How did you stop him?' Yasmine enquired but Miss Sissins acted like she didn't hear the question.

'It was never a good idea. Our agency definitely should have stayed silent and worked undercover as it had done for decades, any attention brought to us could have been catastrophic. Can you imagine, these heroes saving the world one minute and then demanding praise after it? It wouldn't be long until it went to their heads and when they thought they weren't getting enough thanks, they would just refuse to do it. Then, eventually, a foe comes along that can't be stopped because our agents got too distracted by these other things.'

Sophie was getting hooked now. Miss Sissins was clearly getting something off her chest that had been there for a while. She looked over at Yasmine; she was now clearly as engrossed as she was. It also felt to Sophie like Miss Sissins was telling her a story that her dad would have been proud of and would love to hear and that excited her even more.

'That is partly where The Departure, as you call it, came from,' she then said and Sophie and Yasmine carried on listening with great interest.

'The implant had just been devised and all agents had been administered one but me, Mr Houghton and Mr King. We all had a slightly modified version with slightly better software. Mr King could see that the agents were starting an uprising to change the way his company was run and he hated that – he likes to be in control.'

'Go on…' Sophie prompted.

'The agents continued to argue that they should be credited and rewarded and Mr King continued to get nervous that they would take over so it was decided that the agents should be 'uploaded' to the server at Stratus. Their bodies would vanish and their consciences backed up until a day when we deemed it right for them to come back.'

'So, they are still alive?' Sophie asked.

Miss Sissins didn't respond to that question.

'The day then came when an unstoppable force that had taken over so many planets in the universe arrived on Earth and the agency was so divided that there was no way to defeat it using agents. Mr King told me to flick the switch to seal off the planet.'

'Meaning what?' Sophie asked

'The agents were uploaded,' Miss Sissins replied.

'And this was…' Yasmine began.

'10 years ago,' Sophie finished off for her.

'The Departure wasn't just mythicals, girls,' Miss Sissins explained, 'it was all the agents that were assigned to stop them as well.'

There was a moment of reflection from Miss Sissins and the two girls. Sophie's mind was riddled with questions but she didn't know which one to pick first.

'It was me, I… made them disappear… it was my fault and I have to live with that shame,' Miss Sissins concluded.

'Why shame?' Sophie asked, sensitively.

'Because I made a mistake in my coding, the agents weren't uploaded to Stratus like they should have been. They are lost in the system and there is no way to find out where.'

Sophie and Yasmine were disappointed to realise that this thread of the story wasn't going any further yet.

'So, mythicals are still here somewhere?' Sophie asked.

Miss Sissins nodded, 'Yes, they are just all in hiding but we have no idea where. The Departure uploaded and lost the agents but emitted an ear-piercing pulse that caused immense pain and suffering to the mythical creatures. There was nobody to protect the Earth so we had to limit the threats.'

Sophie was fascinated and appalled by this. For the last ten years, mythical creatures had been forced to hide away because of the actions of humanity. It wasn't up to humans to decide who should live on the planet and who shouldn't.

'Can they ever come back?' Yasmine asked.

Miss Sissins looked across the table at the two girls and stared them straight in the eye, 'Yes,' she replied.

'But hang on,' Sophie said, confused, 'the biggest threat ever arrived on Earth. Surely the world is better off with a divided agency than no agency at all? Why not keep the agents? Who stopped this threat?'

'In order to prevent the alien threat from taking over Earth, the final stage of The Departure was to place a huge force field around the Earth. This stops anyone from out in the cosmos getting in and anyone on Earth getting out, 'Miss Sissins answered, 'It's why the sky is the shade of blue that it is – it never used to be like that!'

'So, nobody stopped it? It's still out there?' Sophie guessed, 'And that's why Clara has been dragged into this.'

'And us two!' Yasmine added.

'The force field around the Earth and the pulse being emitted were never meant to last this long and they could fail at any moment meaning the mythicals would come back and cause untold damage and harm. Not only that but, there are aliens out there who would also mean to do us damage. This threat is about to appear again and Mr King still won't release the agents because he thinks he has a better way.'

Sophie quickly surmised that the immediate return of a group of angry, mythical creatures and aliens would not be a good thing for humanity and moved on to her next question.

'So, why is Mr Houghton here, at this school?' asked Sophie.

'Because he wants children to run the agency and he is recruiting,' Miss Sissins replied.

'Ok,' Sophie replied, 'but he doesn't look old enough to be a founding member from decades ago? He looks about ten or twenty years too young?'

'Because he got put in that body,' Miss Sissins said.

'Pardon?' Yasmine chortled.

'I had modified his implant a few days prior to The Departure when I had run tests and refined it. I was told by Mr King to take control of it from the Stratus tower in London and so I used the implant he had to project a different appearance onto his body. This would hide him away from the rest of society and nobody would believe he was who he claimed to be.'

Sophie and Yasmine rocked on their chairs and laughed. 'You had me up until that point. There's no such gadget that makes a person wearing an implant look different. You can't just change something from one thing to another...' Yasmine was cut off at that point.

Miss Sissins had touched behind her ear, under the arm of her glasses and immediately she disappeared and was replaced by Amelia – Sophie's mum, 'Isn't there?' she asked.

The girls nearly fell off their chairs, partly because of shock and partly because they were rocking. They just stared at Amelia, who was now in front of them where Miss Sissins had been seconds earlier. There was still an extremely small part of them that still hadn't believed what Miss Sissins had been saying, but, seeing this with their own eyes right in front of them, implied that it was all true.

'Mum?' Sophie reached out, not breaking eye contact with her.

'No, it's still me,' it was Amelia's voice but it wasn't her. Something wasn't quite right. 'Would you like another one?'

'No thank...' Yasmine started.

Amelia touched behind her ear again and immediately changed into a short, stumpy man with receding, mousey-coloured hair, huge freckles and massive red glasses.

'Who are you now?' asked Sophie.

'This is what Mr Houghton, your head teacher, actually looked like before he tried to start an uprising and I trapped him in that body,' Miss Sissins in the guise of the man in front of them said.

'I recognise you from somewhere,' Yasmine contemplated.

'You will do,' Miss Sissins replied, 'this is the body of Dale Natan.'

'I know that name,' Sophie said, looking towards the top corner of the room in deep thought.

Miss Sissins looked at the pair of them, waiting for the penny to drop about where they had heard the name and seen the face before.

It took Yasmine about five seconds, 'You were Alton King's partner at Shadow and you disappeared years ago!' she shouted like she had got an answer right on a quiz show.

'Yes and, as I said, Mr King needs to do some more explaining to you,' Dale Natan said while morphing back into Miss Sissins 'let him explain the next step.'

'Break has already overrun by two minutes, the class will be coming back in any second,' Yasmine realised.

'Don't worry Yazz; I can slow down time for everyone but us using the implants,' Miss Sissins looked at her and smiled a huge smile; she put her hands in her pockets and wandered over to her desk.

Sophie and Yasmine both screeched after being astonished for a few seconds. 'WHAT!'

Worryingly, they both now believed her, but something was still troubling Sophie, 'How does Clara fit into all this?' she asked.

'What about that threat you spoke about? The greatest one Earth had ever faced? Is that still out there?'

'You'll see,' said Miss Sissins not even bothering to turn and look at them, 'but first, you're about to go and rescue Clara from wherever she is and hopefully we can do something about the force field back around the Earth and prevent the mythicals from coming back and taking revenge! Oh, and there's the prison as well…'

Chapter 15 – Shadow

Miss Sissins took something small, white and round out of her desk and threw it to Sophie. It looked like a tiny, plain white marble or a miniature table tennis ball and was completely smooth as Sophie rolled it around in her hand.

'Put that on the side of your head Sophie, just sort of in between your eyebrow and your ear.'

Sophie looked at Yasmine who just shrugged her shoulders.

'Don't I need one?' Yasmine asked.

'No Yazz, I'm going to send you a link through your implant. You just need to open it when it comes through.'

Yasmine did that look that everyone logging into the implant did and zoned out. Sophie meanwhile was still playing with the ball.

'Is this because I don't have an implant?' she asked.

'Of course, you've got one. You just fainted while it was being installed. It needs help to finish its installation or it won't work.'

'But all the lights went red?' Sophie asked.

'We'll get to that in a while. For now, just put that where I told you to,' Miss Sissins explained, almost brushing Sophie's shock at this revelation to one side.

Sophie only thought about putting the contraption on her temple for a few seconds before deciding that it was only going to get weirder so what did it matter?

As soon as the device touched the side of her head, Sophie's mind was sent flying down a road of colour. Lights flashed and other longer beams of light darted out in front of her. It was similar to the lightning that had greeted her when she saw Clara the first time but this seemed a lot smoother and more relaxing. In a matter of seconds, she had stopped and found herself standing next to Miss Sissins and Yasmine in a huge grey, completely empty, warehouse.

Sophie gazed around but could only see walls, ceiling and floor and it was all bland and boring. There was nothing there. She then remembered what Miss Sissins had said about slowing down time so she looked at her watch. It had stopped. She looked over to Yasmine and mimed for her to check hers. Yasmine did so and noticed that hers had stopped too.

'Why have our watches stopped?' Sophie asked.

'They haven't, they're just going really slowly, keep up. You're in the actual Shadow building that has been on the news and where everything is invented and made,' Miss Sissins said this almost like she was stating the obvious and that this kind of thing happened every day.

'How are we here?' Sophie asked.

'You're a projection of your real self, Sophie, an avatar if you like but in the real world. This is the real Shadow HQ but you're a computer-generated version of yourself. I have added a plugin to your implant that allows you to be projected here in 'soft-light'. It gives the impression that you're here because you can interact with people around you and they will believe you are actually there but your real selves are actually still in the classroom.'

Remembering there was nothing in the room, Sophie reached out to touch Yasmine's shoulder but her hand went straight through it – much like it had done with Clara before.

'Why can't I touch anything?' she asked.

'Because you're just a projection. It's similar to the plugin people use to view sports events as if they're actually in the stadium or watching a film in a cinema but, unlike them, you can move around and interact with the people around you, kind of like a hologram projection. However, because you are just basically a clever combination of lights, you can't touch anything. You could, theoretically, pick anywhere on the planet and the implant will project your image and your conscience there so you can walk around. Get it to project you in your living room right now and you could chat with your mum and she would honestly believe it's you. Then you can zone back out and you'll be back in your real body in the classroom,' Miss Sissins explained.

Yasmine finished looking around her and quite simply said 'Well this isn't much to look at is it?'

Miss Sissins rolled her eyes at her and muttered something about younger children having no patience, then, she tapped her ear and said 'It's me, Jane, I've brought them, Sir.'

It was then that Sophie realised she had had no idea what Miss Sissins's first name had been.

'Jane?' she asked.

'Jane Sissins is my real name; I thought about using another but then wondered what the point was. I did think about using John Smith but apparently, that's already taken by some alien with an alter-ego!' she replied.

She touched her ear again, 'Yes, they're both here.'

Out of nowhere, the floor around them started to shake. Out of the ground grew white tubes that covered about five meters in every direction all around Sophie and Yasmine. There were narrow thin ones, huge fat ones and on top of each was an object. Instantly, Sophie noticed that on top of the largest one was a car! It looked like any other self-driving car that the girls were used to seeing on the road – it had one seat at the front if the driver wanted to take over in manual, behind that were the passenger seats where people would sit in a circle and chat like they were in their own living room. What made this car stand out for Sophie though was that this one had blue neon lights inside the front bumper which shone out. These lights then changed to red, then green.

'What are those?' Sophie asked.

'They allow the driver to see in infrared, night vision, heat vision – basically you can see a lot more. Really helpful if you're following someone at night and don't want the lights on,' Miss Sissins replied.

On her left, Yasmine's eyes were drawn to a much smaller tube which had various items of jewellery on it. She walked over and had a look. Each one had a different label. 'Communicator' was written on an earring. 'Camera' was written on a necklace, 'X-ray glasses' on, funnily enough, a pair of glasses.

Sophie scanned even more. There were more of the little white dots that she had put on the side of her head. 'Time dilators – speeds time up for the wearer' read the label underneath them. It sounded a lot more professional than 'small white ball' that she had been referring to it as! Next to them, there were more with a label that read 'Time dilators – slows time down for the wearer'.

On the next tube, the time dilator was missing, Sophie figured that that was what she was wearing.

Before they could look around anymore, a voice calmly and mysteriously said from the other end of the warehouse, 'You've got them.'

Coming towards them was an old-looking man with a shiny head. He had long pointy fingers and a menacing grin. Sophie recognised him immediately; it was Alton King.

'Were you expecting us?' Sophie asked.

'Of course!' King replied, coldly, 'Ever since I gave you both your implants, I thought you would be banging down my door demanding to know why you had seen Clara, but you didn't show up until now!'

'You know Clara?' Yasmine asked, slightly bemused.

'Yes,' King said, seemingly annoyed by the inconvenience of the question, 'she's worked for us for a few months now. But now we've lost her and we aren't sure how we can bring her back. Jane says that you two are two of the most talented young children she's ever met, so we are putting all our faith in you.'

King walked up to Sophie and studied her carefully. It was just as creepy as the first time they'd met on the stage.

'An excellent, realistic projection Jane, well done, these two could trick their own parents into thinking these were their real daughters,' he commented.

'That's what I said,' Miss Sissins said, seemingly wanting to please King.

'If you could access your implant Sophie, you should have a message there waiting from Clara,' King said, sounding as close to excited as she had seen him.

Sophie looked confused. 'I'm sure I don't have an implant; the implant didn't work when you did it on stage. I passed out before you could put it in.'

King looked at Miss Sissins. 'Of course, you have one.'

'I have told her,' Miss Sissins said.

'Everything that morning went almost exactly as Clara had planned,' King said, 'it's just we didn't act or realise quickly enough.'

'You caused me to faint in front of billions of people, making me the most famous 10-year-old on Earth. That was what was meant to happen?' Sophie was getting cross.

'No, Clara caused you to faint all in an effort to help find her. You didn't get the message the first time because she made a miscalculation which caused you to faint. So, she hacked into the whole implant mainframe in Stratus and gave you a message which meant that every user on Earth was overloaded with information for 60 seconds and as a result caused them all to pass out,' King replied dismissively.

'Clara wouldn't do that to me! It's horrible!' Sophie wasn't having it and stormed off through the lines of equipment that now adorned the warehouse.

Yasmine made a move to go and follow her but Miss Sissins put her hand in front of her to get her to stop and shook her head. Miss Sissins then followed Sophie and caught up with her. She walked around in front of her and saw that the news that her cousin had supposedly done her harm was quite distressing.

'This was all I ever wanted. I'm clever; I can use the implant for amazing things. I screamed at my dad the other day because I couldn't have one. It wasn't even his fault! Now, I apparently have one but only because I'm needed to help get my cousin back! I wanted one but not because I wanted to be used.'

Miss Sissins understood completely.

'Why couldn't you have just invited me here to have an implant fitted? My mum and dad clearly knew about it because they were at school on Tuesday watching it happen.'

'Soph, we don't even let cleaners into this place, let alone children and their parents. Yesterday, you must have seen on the news all those people flocking to interview Mr King. They were here partly for answers to the questions about the fainting, but also on the off chance that they might get invited in. That will never happen. If word got out that we had invited children and parents into the building, the press would be all over you anyway. You would have been famous and the press would assume you knew what was happening. By putting you on stage and feeding the cameras and the media the information, we had control over it and nobody comes into Shadow. The only person that matters at the end of all this is Clara. We need her back!'

Sophie sort of understood. She could see why she hadn't been invited. Nobody had been inside Shadow for years. Sophie now knew why. The gates had been locked ten years ago and nobody ever went through them because there wasn't anything that King had wanted them to see.

Sophie spent a few more minutes talking to Miss Sissins then, eventually, came back.

'Clara is all that matters? Am I free to go once she comes back if I want?' Sophie asked.

'If that's what you want,' King replied, 'although I can see you doing great things. If there is one thing that Dale and I almost agree on it's that children are very much the future of this agency.'

'What do I have to do?' Sophie asked, slightly more excited by the adventure they were about to go on.

'Nothing, just stand still while I activate this implant for you seeing as you have been unable to do it yourself.'

King pulled something out of his pocket; it looked like a sort of magic wand with multi-coloured, flashing lights. He flicked a switch on it and pointed it at Sophie's avatar.

'This should be able to finish the installation as I can use your projection to communicate with your implant in your classroom,' King said.

A weight seemed to be lifted from her mind. Sophie felt light-headed and so sat herself down on the floor. Something felt different, but good different. She shook her head to compose herself then it occurred to her what she had to do. She looked forwards but not at anything in particular, just the air in front of her. Everything turned white apart from the flashing red dot and now, next to it, the words 'You have one new message.'

Excitement gripped Sophie; she had what she wanted – a functioning implant. For a few seconds, the revelation that the red light that had been plaguing her since yesterday was a message (presumably from Clara) faded into insignificance, Sophie could now do what she wanted with her life. Living with next to nothing was no longer an issue for her and, now it was working, she briefly forgot that the only reason she had one was because she was being used. She had a way to escape the difficult aspects of her life and make it better. That feeling didn't last long though.

'Sophie, can you hear me?'

Sophie realised straight away that it was King and looked through the implant display and back into reality. Yasmine, Miss Sissins and King came back into focus.

'Yes, it worked. I have a message,' Sophie told them.

King and Miss Sissins smiled with relief, 'It must be Clara with her location,' King said, 'open it.'

'Not until you tell me exactly what is going on,' Sophie replied, sharply, 'I've heard part of it from Miss Sissins, now I want to hear it from you.' Sophie knew she held all the power in this scenario and wasn't scared to use it.

King stepped back at this; he wasn't used to being spoken to like that. Yasmine smirked behind Sophie, proud of her friend for standing up to King and not just caving in and doing exactly what he said. King then looked at Miss Sissins, who just shrugged as if to tell him that he didn't have a choice and that Sophie wouldn't budge until she knew exactly what was happening and how they had got here.

Chapter 16 – How Did We Get Here?

Eventually, King started to tell Sophie everything and Sophie kept recapping the story in her mind…

He had secretly run an agency that stopped the mythicals in the olden days from taking over the Earth. His partner, Dale Natan, had run it along with him and they had operated in complete secrecy. Natan decided that this was unfair and that the agents who were risking their lives should be praised and recognised by the people they were saving. King didn't like this idea; he believed that it would do the agency no good whatsoever to open its doors like that.

Natan continued his quest though and got all the other agents on his side. Miss Sissins had sensed that they were close to going public and, in order to protect the agency's secrets, set about putting in a failsafe should the agents go too far, which King had agreed to. This failsafe came in three forms: the very first implants that were administered to agents in order to be able to upload them if they went too far (at this point, King would have done literally anything to protect his company), a protective shield that would cut the world off from the rest of the universe and an ear-splitting sound wave that would send every mythical creature into hiding as there would now be nobody to stop them doing whatever they wanted.

Just a few days after the final agent had been implanted, Shadow received word that the worst threat the world had ever faced had arrived from beyond the stars and the agents demanded recognition from the public in order to stop it. Sensing a catastrophic mutiny from his agents that would cost the planet everything, King instructed Miss Sissins to activate the failsafe.

Within a few minutes of flicking the switch, the defensive shield had been dropped to stop the invasion. To the best of their knowledge, every mythical creature had been sent into hiding and every agent had been wiped out in one go.

At the disappearance of the agents, Dale Natan was livid. He knew that King and Miss Sissins had done it on purpose to stop him from going public with them. Before he could do anything more, Miss Sissins had used Natan's own implant against him and trapped him in a different body using the first plugin of its kind, meaning nobody would believe he was who he said he was.

With no mythical creatures to protect the world from, and the Shadow corporation making infinite amounts of money by selling the updated implant, which wasn't affected by The Departure, the three were at a loss as to what to do. They knew the shield around the Earth and pulse wouldn't last forever but also that the agents were gone for good as nobody knew exactly where they had been uploaded to. It was like their consciences had been lost in the uploading process. They existed but were lost in an infinite line of code. So, they needed a plan for the day when the return came as none of them knew how to bring the agents back. Natan had suspected that King did know where they were but would never get that information out of him.

In a few years, Earth would be opened up to visitors beyond the stars again and mythical creatures would be free to roam the land once more if something wasn't done.

After a few years of discussion, the three of them agreed that the best way to bring the agency back would be to use children as agents rather than adults. The reasoning behind the three's opinions though was very different. Natan thought that children would be more fame and fortune hungry than adults, and so would find it very easy to manipulate them to eventually get the recognition he felt he deserved. Miss Sissins and King however thought completely the opposite – that children were morally stronger and more aware of the need for secrecy and subtlety. King just questioned whether children could handle the complexity of how to complete missions and worried that leaving the responsibility in such young, inexperienced hands might be dangerous for the planet and wasn't completely convinced that children would keep his beloved company and legacy safe. As a result of their many disagreements, Natan left and Miss Sissins and King continued to run Shadow and give the people of the world what they wanted.

Not long after the split, Miss Sissins decided that if they were going to start using children in a few years when the shield failed, then they had better start recruiting some. At the same time, Natan had the same idea. He had settled down, married and had a son of his own and started a career as a teacher, quickly working his way up to being a head. Following him into the profession, Miss Sissins knew exactly where to start looking for children – the small village of Pinkleton in the middle of England. King didn't understand but Miss Sissins insisted they should look at using a young girl at school called Clara as Jane said she had 'a skillset that no other child would have,' King saw no reason to argue but said that they must wait until Clara was older. Natan also started at Pinkleton on the same day as Miss Sissins but under the guise of Mr Houghton. He knew there must have been a reason that Jane would start there but didn't know what it was. Miss Sissins didn't see it as a problem and agreed with King that this was the perfect way to keep an eye on Natan.

Once she was reaching the end of year 5, Clara was brought in as the first agent – giving the three remaining members of Shadow time to train her up before they brought in even more children.

Clara impressed immediately in all the tests she was given but didn't completely blow the adults away. Miss Sissins claimed she had a natural talent for it and King could see she knew more than she was letting on. Natan had pressed Clara for how much of a desire she had to want to be rich and famous but she clearly wasn't the sort of child and she had morals and ideas that aligned a lot more with Miss Sissins and King.

Annoyed that Clara wouldn't give him what he wanted, and with Miss Sissins and King unwilling to take on any more children yet, Natan had hijacked not just Clara's implant but her dads' as well. He hid them away from Miss Sissins and King and only agreed to let her free if he could give an implant to his own son, who he was sure would follow in his footsteps and desire fame and fortune over everything else. Backed into a corner, Miss Sissins and King agreed to give Reuben an implant but only if other children of *their* choosing could also be given one. The three agreed and so the competition was announced at school as a cover. King contacted Sophie's and Yasmine's parents through Miss Sissins and all was set up.

All was going as King, Miss Sissins and Natan wanted, until, Sophie's implantation when Clara had attempted to break through and contact her, inadvertently causing Sophie to faint and become the face of the whole process. Natan had been determined that the honour should have befallen his son so that he could start drawing attention to him. It was when Natan saw Sophie leave school that day, to a barrage of reporters, that he realised that nobody was interested in his son and so he refused to give up Clara's location to Miss Sissins and King. He had well and truly gone back on the deal. Without proof that his story was true, Natan had nothing and was therefore holding Clara hostage until he had decided what to do next.

So, there they all now were. Waiting to find out what Clara's message said to Sophie.

'That's some story,' Sophie said, desperately trying to keep up with it all.

'I think I need to hear it again,' Yasmine added, quite confused.

Sophie had followed it well and now understood a lot more than before, so she zoned back into the implant and clicked on the message icon by looking at it and blinking twice. The screen faded then reappeared as a satellite map with a pin in one of the buildings, next to the pin was an envelope icon. Sophie looked at it and blinked twice. It opened and simply said, 'Help.'

'It's a map,' Sophie said, without zoning back out.

She heard King's voice, 'Send it to me so I can work out where she is.'

Sophie though didn't need to. She knew exactly where this message had come from, she recognised the map.

'She's at home?' she said, sounding confused.

'Send it to me,' King repeated.

Sophie closed the programs and clicked the share button. As a result, the white tubes disappeared and the map was uploaded onto a large monitor that simply appeared out of the floor and positioned itself in front of the four people in the room.

'But that doesn't make sense,' Sophie said, zoning back into the real world, 'why would she still be at home? She left six weeks ago.'

'I don't know,' Miss Sissins replied, 'We need to go there and find out.'

Sophie was determined now, she knew where her cousin was and wanted desperately to go and fetch her.

'We can't right now,' Miss Sissins said, 'break time is nearly over. We need to get back.'

'Sorry?' Yasmine said, incredulously, 'we have to go back and do English and grammar before we can go and rescue Clara?'

Miss Sissins nodded. 'Pretty much, that's how it works. Ever since we lost all of our agents, things have to take their time.'

'That's ridiculous. You need more agents,' said Yasmine, still not quite believing what she was hearing.

'Well yes, Miss Ariti, why do you think you two are here and Clara is out there?' King added, 'Like I said, I tried doing this with adults, they got obsessed with the idea of payment and fame. I meant what I said on the stage at your school. Children *are* one of the greatest assets on this planet and for too long they have been ignored by too many people. When I relaunch this agency, I want the best agents I can muster – children. Children carry themselves in a better way than adults. They know the difference between right and wrong and do their best to stand up for everyone else and not put themselves first.'

Yasmine looked decidedly unimpressed, 'Bit cheesy don't you think?' she asked with a smirk.

Sophie and Miss Sissins nodded. King tutted and grumbled to himself.

'So, what do you think you two? Care to help rescue Clara?' Miss Sissins asked with excitement in her voice.

'YES!' they both replied.

'…after English and grammar?' Miss Sissins concluded.

This time Yasmine and Sophie's 'yes' was a lot more subdued.

'Do we get to be full agents?' Yasmine asked, 'Save the world and protect millions of innocent people?'

'We will see about that, you'll have to prove to Mr King that you're capable. That's the one doubt he has. Make him question you and he will soon get rid of you. Nothing will make him risk his company,' Miss Sissins added, 'but hopefully, after English when we've rescued Clara, I can bring you back here and give you the proper tour.'

'Can we keep our codenames?' Yasmine asked.

'No,' Miss Sissins replied, instantly.

Despite the rejection, Yasmine and Sophie still looked incredibly excited. Sophie couldn't have imagined in her wildest dreams that something like this was going to happen. Her fantasies were coming true albeit not in the way she had imagined but long may it continue she thought to herself. She now had an implant and was going to make the most of it! She might have been used but right now there were people, not least her cousin, who needed her help.

Miss Sissins explained to Yasmine and Sophie how to deactivate the time dilator plugin and the three of them found themselves back in the classroom - the clock showing just thirty seconds after they had left. Sophie put the white ball to one side as Miss Sissins left the room to go and get the rest of the class, Yasmine and Sophie got their stuff ready for English. This was going to be a long lesson!

Chapter 17 – English and Grammar

The rest of the class came streaming in after break time like cattle into a shed. They all found their places and got their English books out. Yasmine and Sophie had already done so in the minute or two they had before everyone came in so they sat back and thought about what they were going to do next. They whispered to each other as quietly as they could but it wasn't long before Katie, who was now sat in the seat that Miss Sissins had sat in earlier, started talking to them.

'Where were you at break?' she asked.

'We were in here, talking to Miss Sissins and Mr Houghton,' Yasmine had bent the truth slightly but in a way what she was saying was true.

'I was talking to Mr Houghton for the last part of break so that can't be true,' Katie said, suspiciously, 'he came out onto the playground to talk to me.'

Sophie and Yasmine thought back to the last time they saw Mr Houghton, who they now knew as Dale Natan. It felt like ages ago when they had confronted him in his office but, in actuality, it had been less than ten minutes ago.

'What did he talk about?' Sophie asked shadily.

Katie couldn't reply, Miss Sissins was asking the class to turn the noise down and make sure they had written the date. The opportunity for conversation was gone; this came both as a relief and a disappointment to Yasmine and Sophie who, while they didn't want to face a grilling from Katie about where they had been, did want to ask Katie more about the recurring chats she seemed to be having with Mr Houghton. Couple together today's chat at break time with yesterday's, when almost everyone else had gone home, and Sophie realised that Mr Houghton was probably up to something.

For the next hour and a half, Sophie's mind was racing. She couldn't concentrate on the recount of what she did over the summer holidays at all because of what had happened in the two-and-a-bit days since they finished, which was obviously a lot more exciting. Sophie had no holiday to write about, no exciting trips out she could recap, she had spent most of the six weeks with her nose in a book trying desperately to better herself. The other part of the holiday she had spent either playing out with Yasmine and Katie or missing Clara.

Almost all of Sophie's thoughts were taken up with the unanswered questions that she still had. What was Mr Houghton planning? Why hadn't Miss Sissins fainted yesterday? How and why was Clara still at home?

The 90 minutes dragged and Sophie had only written two lines. Occasionally, Yasmine would try and talk to her or Katie but Miss Sissins was on them like a shot and got them to stop talking. Never had a lesson seemed so insignificant. Sophie looked over at Yasmine's work – she seemed to be the same – barely written anything.

At 11:55, the classroom door swung open and in walked Mr Houghton. He scanned the room and seemed to linger when he saw Yasmine and Sophie. He then walked round looking at each child's work in turn, not talking to any of them. Sophie and Yasmine simply kept their heads down and carried on pretending to work. They were both nervous as to what Mr Houghton was doing. He quite often came into lessons to see how children were getting on and what they were learning but this felt different.

As the clock ticked round to 11:59, Mr Houghton showed no sign of leaving. Sophie and Yasmine were now both sweating with nerves. At 12:00 the bell went and all the students started tidying up.

Mr Houghton stopped them mid-tidying and said, 'Miss Sissins, I must say, I am incredibly impressed with what the year sixes have produced in this lesson. They really have done some top writing, even though they have only been back for a few days.'

'Why thank you Mr Houghton. They've all been working extremely hard,' Miss Sissins replied, shuffling slightly uncomfortably.

'There are though a few students who haven't done quite as much as the rest and I think they should probably spend some time with me over dinner time to try and catch up with the others,' Mr Houghton said, with evil undertones.

Miss Sissins worked out very quickly what was going on and looked straight at Yasmine and Sophie, who had paused mid-tidying to listen to what Mr Houghton had to say.

'Oh, I think they have all worked extremely hard,' Miss Sissins replied, without taking her eyes off Sophie and Yasmine.

'Oh no, I disagree, if you look here, Tyler has done a page and a half and Kyle has done two full pages. Even Ryan, if he doesn't mind me saying, has done an excellent job.'

Ryan was the worst behaved boy in school and barely did anything except be horrible to people and he never seemed to get any praise so Sophie and Yasmine now knew for certain that something wasn't right! On top of that, Kyle and Tyler were two of the boys that sat towards the front of the class and weren't too clever. They both stood there beaming that they had been picked out by the head teacher for working hard. Little did they know his real reasons for doing do.

Yasmine and Sophie were starting to panic; they looked down on their four lines and five lines respectively and began to dread what

Mr Houghton was inevitably going to say next. They couldn't stay in at dinner, they had Clara to rescue.

Mr Houghton carried on, 'However, some girls over there,' he pointed in Sophie and Yasmine's vague direction, 'have done nowhere near that much. Therefore, I think some time with me over dinner time won't go amiss... Miss.'

Miss Sissins was lost for words and couldn't think of a defence and had to agree with Mr Houghton or risk making a scene in the classroom surrounded by year 6 children.

'Therefore, I would like to borrow you over dinner time, to get you to finish your writing, it isn't like you had anything more exciting to do over dinner, is it?' Mr Houghton began, 'Come with me – Sophie and Yasmine... and Katie.'

Chapter 18 – In at Dinner

Plans scuppered and feeling helpless, Sophie and Yasmine were once again marching down the corridor at school. This time though they were heading *towards* Mr Houghton's office not away from it. Surely he had realised what they had been up to and was now going to prevent them from going to look for Clara on their lunch break. On top of that, poor Katie was being dragged along now with no prior knowledge of anything. Their original plan for lunchtime was certainly over.

Panicked, Sophie began to imagine what kind of hellish torture Mr Houghton might have in store for them if, as Miss Sissins had explained and King had backed up, he was one of the most dangerous men in the known worlds.

Eventually they reached the end of the corridor and Mr Houghton's lumbering figure turned the handle to his office door.

Mrs Tabard, who was on her way out to do dinner duty, tutted and said, 'Are you staying in again girls?'

Mr Houghton replied, 'Oh nothing serious, Mrs T.'

She then scurried off to go and take care of a spillage in the dining hall.

All three girls carried their English books and a pen; however, they knew their punishment was going to be much worse than having to write a few extra lines at least Sophie and Yasmine did. And what of Clara, who knew what kind of mess she was in and how much longer she could survive?

A drip of sweat appeared on Sophie's forehead and trickled down. Nervous, the three girls lined up next to Mr Houghton's desk and waited to see what was coming their way. Mr Houghton sat down on his huge chair and leant over to the side of his desk to open a drawer. Sophie began to wonder what possible implement a man as dangerous as Mr Houghton would use on people that had gone behind his back. Sophie and Yasmine just stood next to his desk petrified, Katie still just looked confused.

'Sit down,' Mr Houghton said in a deep voice.

Sophie had never found his voice threatening or scary before but, right now, it reverberated around her ears like a never-ending thunder clap.

The girls sat on the spare seats, all of them looking solemnly at the floor. Mr Houghton took something out of his drawer and closed it gently. He was taking the lid off something and with a pop he succeeded.

Within an instant Mr Houghton had picked up his equipment of impending doom and spun round on his chair.

'Biscuit…' he offered.

Sophie and Yasmine simply stared in the tub and were faced with nothing except for a selection of biscuits for them to choose from. Without waiting to be asked twice, Katie reached out and took one. Yasmine sat there, speechless. Sophie was desperate to say 'Phew' but couldn't bring herself to. Her heart was pounding like a race horse in her chest, she half expected it to burst out at any second.

'No thank you,' Yasmine squeaked.

Sophie merely shook her head, not taking her eyes of the biscuits.

'Don't you like them?' Mr Houghton asked.

'Not hungry,' was Sophie's reply.

'Oh, that's a shame, it's dinner time and you don't want anything. Never mind,' Mr Houghton put the lid back on and put the tub back in his desk. He spun back round again.

'We all know why we're here,' Mr Houghton began.

Katie nodded and started taking her pen out of her pocket, went to start writing but then slowly put it back when she saw that no one else had taken theirs out. Sophie and Yasmine stayed rigid.

'I don't know what Miss Sissins has told you girls but I assure you it isn't how it happened and I am not who she says I am,' Mr Houghton said in a tone completely unfamiliar to the girls.

'She said you're greedy and you want to be applauded for doing your duty!' Sophie began, 'You want street parades and huge celebrations just for doing your job. Police officers, fire fighters and loads of others keep people safe but you got everyone to think that you're better than them and that you and your workers should be treated differently,' Sophie finished her rant; Yasmine had turned to look at her with a look of 'I didn't know you had it in you.'

'And...' Mr Houghton replied.

This bamboozled Sophie. She had been expecting a huge tirade of shouting and screaming and general evilness, but it didn't come. As a result, she had to think on her feet.

'It's wrong,' was the best she could come up with.

'It's wrong for brave men and women to want to be recognised for risking their lives? Police officers and fire fighters, to use your example, can get their names in the papers or medals and they certainly get paid a whole lot more than my agents did. The people I worked with got next to nothing,' Mr Houghton remained extremely calm; he had clearly used this argument many times before.

Sophie had no come back to this, Yasmine was lost for words and Katie didn't seem to have a clue what anyone was talking about. So, the three girls stayed quiet.

'Has Miss Sissins told you about the inventions and technology that are available at Shadow?' Mr Houghton asked, slightly changing the subject. 'There is technology in there that could put an end to world hunger, poverty could become a thing of the past, men, women and children all over the world don't need to die unnecessarily. But King has destroyed most of it because they needed people to operate them, all in an effort to stop my people from being recognised. He was, and still is, wrong,' His tone was getting decidedly darker. 'We could change the world for the better but he won't risk that company of his!'

'We've seen some of it,' Yasmine said.

'Then you know there are incredible things there. Life-changing things, world changing things and King won't share them. All I wanted was for people on Earth to be better off and looked after – my agents included. But King and his unwillingness to allow those that did such an amazing job to be recognised and rewarded stopped all that.'

There were clearly things that Miss Sissins and King hadn't told Yasmine and Sophie. That or Mr Houghton was lying. However, he had that same look on his face and passion in his voice that Miss Sissins had had when she was telling her version of events. The truth must have been part way between the two.

Sophie weighed up what she had heard, 'There must have been a downside to all these solutions. King wouldn't have just stopped you because he didn't want you to be famous.'

'Not that I know of, ask King and Miss Sissins yourself. King said there was a risk of some of the agents getting a bit carried away with their popularity, but I had faith in them. I just wished King had shared the same confidence and allowed them to try.'

Upon hearing this, Sophie began to feel torn. If there were solutions to all these problems (starvation, poverty to name just two) then why were Miss Sissins and King holding back? It didn't make sense; surely it was worth the risk of some agents becoming famous?

'Conflicted, aren't you?' Mr Houghton asked.

Surprisingly it was Yasmine who jumped in while Sophie sat still, deep in thought. 'No, I don't think you've told us everything. You're not telling us something.'

'Yasmine, I am keeping nothing from you,' Mr Houghton was back to being his calm self and Sophie found herself believing him.

She remained deep in thought while Yasmine kept probing.

'Why choose us? Why did we get an implant? You keep taking about a competition; that was all you,' she exclaimed.

'Just because King and I disagree on this thing doesn't mean we disagree on everything. We agreed that if the agency was to be rebuilt, it would be with children at the core. In the conversations that Sissins, King and I have had we have all agreed that. The three of us also agreed that it would be Clara first, followed by you two. I'm sure Sissins and King told you this.'

'Not exactly,' Yasmine replied, 'what about Reuben?'

'He's my son; I wanted him to have the best. Getting King to agree to him having an implant wasn't difficult when I told him I would return Clara. He ruined that though when Clara tried to contact you, Sophie. She and King clearly had something they were hiding, some hidden plan, trying to ruin me and get her out without me knowing,' Mr Houghton relaxed on his chair; he was certainly convinced of everything he was saying. 'See Yasmine, I have nothing to hide. Ask me anything and I will tell you the truth. You are the future, on that we all agree, but, it would be better under my guidance not that ancient King or that maverick Sissins. They can make you good, I can make you legends,' Mr Houghton said.

'Where's Clara?' Sophie finally snapped out of her deep thoughts. She knew the answer and so did Yasmine, but Mr Houghton didn't know that she knew. This would be the perfect way to test if he was lying.

'Pardon, Sophie?'

'Where is Clara?' Sophie asked again at lot more impatiently.

'She's at home, where she has been for the past six weeks.'

Mr Houghton's answer matched what Sophie and Yasmine had found out at Shadow not two hours ago.

'Why?' asked Sophie.

'She is lying perfectly safe on her bed Sophie; physically she is more than fine. Mentally though, time is definitely not on her side, shall we say? Take her back, I won't stop you, it's been fun watching her suffer and she is not much use to me now anyway. Reuben is definitely ready to become famous, then I can have everything I ever wanted,' Mr Houghton was reaching new levels of deceitfulness – using his own son to achieve his personal goals.

Sophie jumped up from the seat and grabbed Yasmine's hand, 'Come on, I know what's happening with Clara and what he's done to her.'

Reaching out for the door handle, Sophie heard Mr Houghton say one final thing.

'If you do start to see things more from my perspective do come and find me.'

Katie stayed sat down, not invited by her friends, who had left her. She just asked Mr Houghton 'Do I still need to finish this?' showing him her English book.

'Yes...' Mr Houghton said but Sophie heard nothing more as the door to his office closed.

Yasmine and Sophie ran down the corridor towards the classroom. When they reached it, they threw open the door and Sophie immediately shouted at Miss Sissins.

'I know why we haven't heard from Clara. I know what's happening to her! We have to go...now!'

'Do you? We can't go now. There's no safe place to zone out,' Miss Sissins said, frantically.

Sophie sounded very grown up when she replied with, 'There has to be, every second is making a difference to Clara. We have to go, now!'

Sophie was fired up now. She glared at Miss Sissins for trying to stop her from finding Clara. If she had been a bit more disrespectful and disobedient she would have just walked out of school and gone to Clara's house to get her. It was an impossible choice! On the one hand she wanted nothing more than to go around to her cousin's house and help her, on the other, she knew that the amount of trouble she would be in both with school and her parents would be incredible. Being only 10, Sophie still had lots of respect for authority and although she knew Miss Sissins wasn't preventing her because she wanted to, she couldn't help but feel annoyed at her lack of determination.

'Time dilators?' Yasmine asked, 'surely we have the time.'

Miss Sissins looked apologetic, 'Where are we going to zone out? We got away with it at break time because we were only gone for thirty seconds real time. Mr Houghton might have known what we were doing but he never had time to get to the classroom to stop us. We could be gone for a few minutes this time. What if an infant child comes in the classroom sees us on the chairs, and tells Mr Houghton we've fainted like yesterday? The consequences of that could be catastrophic. Not only that but Mr Houghton now knows what we're up to and could just walk in and bring us round!'

'We seriously can't go and rescue Clara because of the possibility of some five-year-old coming in the room?' Yasmine asked.

'Correct Yazz, if we could guarantee to be back in seconds, no problem but we can't be sure of that,' Miss Sissins replied.

Yasmine shook her head in disbelief and Sophie's breathing was getting deeper and the frustration was really building up inside her.

Behind her, the door opened and Katie started to say, 'What was all that…'

'GET OUT!' Sophie screamed at her.

Katie sheepishly closed the door and walked back up the corridor with tears in her eyes. Yasmine made for the door to go after her but Sophie interjected again.

'Leave her, you're with us. We need to work out what to do.'

Yasmine wasn't used to being bossed about and so tutted and gave Sophie a bit of a dirty look. Fortunately, Sophie didn't notice her; she was too deep in thought.

'Where exactly is Clara?' Miss Sissins asked.

'She's in her bedroom, lying on her bed according to Mr Houghton,' Sophie snapped, 'right where both the map showed me and where Mr Houghton said she was.'

'He told you she was there?' Miss Sissins replied.

'Yes, he didn't lie to us about that,' Yasmine added.

The three of them stood there in silence for a few seconds before Miss Sissins asked the question that both she and Yasmine were both thinking.

'Why doesn't she just get up?'

'Because she's got one of these on her and can't take it off.'

Sophie reached into her pocket and pulled out the time dilator that Miss Sissins had used on her at break time.

Miss Sissins and Yasmine stared at it for a few seconds and suddenly they both realised what Sophie was talking about.

'She's trapped in one of these with time racing by faster than ours. It might be that one minute for us is a week for Clara. She disappeared six weeks ago; to her it could be six months, six years or six decades!' Sophie was talking unbelievably quickly now.

'What about your uncles?' Yasmine asked.

'Well if they found that time was speeding up, their lives wouldn't make sense. Did I see at Shadow a time dilator that slowed time down for the person wearing it?' Yasmine asked Miss Sissins.

Miss Sissins thought for a second then said, 'Yes, if they have those on, they might think they have only been sat there for about five minutes, when really they have been there for six weeks. They would have no clue that anything was wrong.'

'Why haven't any of them starved or died from lack of water?' Yasmine asked.

'All implants come with a built-in nutrition chip,' Miss Sissins said, 'they would have no clue they were hungry.'

'Why did it look like Clara was in a prison being tested when I saw her?' Sophie asked.

'No idea,' Miss Sissins replied a little less convincingly than she had been speaking before. 'Let's get her and find out. Well, after school.'

Yasmine and Sophie both rolled their eyes but Sophie knew that if she, the most famous 10-year-old on the planet right now, left school early for no reason then someone on the street would spot her, take a photo of her, upload it and all of a sudden people would be following her everywhere, wondering why she wasn't at school as she should be. She would get grounded for the rest of her life!

'Is there no way we can get in touch with her to let her know we're coming?' Sophie asked.

'I'll get King on it now,' Miss Sissins said.

Miss Sissins zoned out and reappeared seconds later.

'Done,' she said.

Yasmine had her thinking face on. It consisted of scrunched up eyes and pursed lips, 'So for Clara time is passing by more quickly but for her dads time is passing really slowly because Mr Houghton attached time dilators to them?' she asked.

Sophie nodded and could see that Yasmine was still deep in thought.

'What are you thinking?' Sophie asked.

'Why didn't you faint yesterday at break time? Mrs Tabard doesn't have an implant, so she was ok, but you clearly have one but you didn't react yesterday,' Yasmine asked, randomly.

Something clicked inside Sophie as she also realised this, she turned and looked at Miss Sissins as if to further prompt her for an answer. They hadn't been confident enough to ask her yesterday but now they knew the full story they had no problems asking her.

'I made some alterations to the coding in my implant. The changes and installations I made make me unreachable. It's like I am off the system. Not even Mr King has tech as good as mine in his. You'll find that if you search for me, I never come up, but, I can reach you. That's why Clara couldn't contact me. Your implants have *some* of my plugins built in, and that is how you, Yazz, managed to use a time dilator at break without having one stuck to your head like Sophie. Yours is built in but only temporarily while I master the coding but that could take months.'

'Why would you not want to be reached?' Yasmine asked.

'If I could be reached, what do you think I would face when I logged in properly? I'll tell you what – a barrage of messages from the avatars of former agents who have been uploaded somewhere that I can get to them, criticising me for doing what I did. I am better off alone! If I knew where they were I could go and get them instantly but I can't and I just can't face their cries.'

Yasmine didn't respond she just nodded. Miss Sissins wasn't being her usual animated self again. Yasmine had touched a nerve and both she and Sophie could see it and decided to leave it well alone.

'So, are we stuck at school for the rest of the day?' Sophie asked quickly changing the subject back again.

'Afraid so' Miss Sissins replied truthfully.

'But Clara could be ageing by the second,' exclaimed Yasmine.

'Her mind might be but her body will be fine. She'll, physically, be a normal 10-year-old whenever we go and get her. Unless we wait until her eleventh birthday…' Miss Sissins was waffling again now.

'OK, we get it,' Sophie said, showing her frustration again.

It was going to be a very long afternoon for the three of them.

Chapter 19 – The Rescue

Sophie and Yasmine had never known an afternoon like it. It dragged in a way like no other lesson the pair had ever been in. They wanted so desperately to get out and go to Clara's but they just couldn't. Miss Sissins had given them the opportunity to go home sick, the problem with that was – first of all Mr Houghton would have to okay it (which wasn't going to happen) and, even if he did okay it, their parents would have to come and fetch them from school so how would they ever get around to Clara's? No, they decided, as painful as it was, they were better off at school studying Genghis Khan and his travels from one country to another trying to impose his ideology onto everyone he found or executing them if they didn't follow him.

The afternoon continued to creep by at a snail's pace. Miss Sissins could see that the pair of them were getting more frustrated. She wandered over to them and whispered that King had somehow got a message to Clara and that she knew they were coming. However, the girls already knew this as King had also sent them a message telling them the same thing. (They had both snuck off to the toilet part way through the afternoon so that they could check their messages without the rest of the class seeing what they were doing.)

Fact after fact after fact about the Mongol leader who travelled through country after country – normally Sophie would be interested but not today. After a while, Sophie had completely switched off from the world around her – Miss Sissins could see the stress she was under and so decided not to tell her off. In her imagination, Sophie was planning what she would do when she eventually got to Clara – hug her? Tell her off for leading this secret life and not telling her trio of friends about any of it? Sophie had no clue what she was going to do.

Five minutes before home time, Miss Sissins sent the children out. The parents, who were used to Miss Sissins sending them out late but never on time let alone early, were staggered and rushed off the playground with their little darlings before Miss Sissins could change her mind and summon them back. The only ones that hung around the classroom afterwards were Sophie, Yasmine and Katie.

'Walk home with you?' Katie asked.

'Err, we want to ask Miss Sissins something. Then I don't think we're going straight home,' Yasmine was again bending the truth.

'You don't want me around, do you?' Katie was getting upset, 'My dad didn't want me and now, not even my two best friends want me! I'll show you!'

Katie stormed out the classroom and up the corridor before anyone could get a word in. Secretly, Yasmine and Sophie were glad she had gone so they didn't have to make the conversation any more awkward or lie to Katie any more than they had already. They were planning on telling her everything but they wanted Clara back first. Right now, Katie would get in the way and just ask too many questions.

After a brief chat with Miss Sissins about the agreed upon plan – Sophie and Yasmine would go and get Clara first then Miss Sissins would use her face-changing tech to go around again later and sort her dads' memories out – Yasmine and Sophie headed for Clara's house. It wasn't too far from Sophie's and between the two houses was the park that the four girls would often go and play on. On the way there, there was the odd snap of a camera that belonged to younger children, taking a picture of Sophie – the adults that wanted to take a photo merely had to use their built-in implant camera so that was less of a distraction for Sophie.

Upon arriving at the house, everything seemed normal. The garden was neatly kept and the house appeared to be deserted. Sophie walked straight up to the living room window of the house and peered in. There was nothing inside. It had been cleared out completely, almost like it was ready to be sold. Racing round the back, Sophie peered in another window but it was the same in the kitchen as it had been in the living room at the front.

Sophie and Yasmine both charged back round to the front of the house to see if there was anything they had missed.

Finding that it was just a perfectly empty, village house, Sophie contacted Miss Sissins, 'There's nothing here,' she said.

'That's not possible,' Miss Sissins replied, 'We know Clara is in there.'

Sophie turned away from the house and zoned into her implant. As she looked at the air in front of her, something leapt across the corner of her eye.

'What was that?' she said to Yasmine.

'What was what?' Yasmine replied.

Sophie turned away so that she was facing up the road at right angles to the front of the house. Something else flashed past the corner of her eye.

'That…' she said, again.

Yasmine looked confused by the apparent hallucinations her friend was having.

'Is it a perception filter?' Miss Sissins asked over the radio.

'A what?' Sophie asked.

'What happens if you zone out while looking at the house? Look at the air in front of it, not directly at it,' Miss Sissins instructed.

Sophie and Yasmine both did as they were instructed and as they looked in front of the house a completely different picture was painted.

The grass was overgrown to at least twice the height of Sophie and Yasmine. Litter had been thrown onto the path up to the house and from what the girls could see the house itself was in a huge state of disrepair.

'It's a tip!' Yasmine exclaimed.

'That's a perception filter,' Miss Sissins began to explain, 'Mr Houghton has put one over the house so that anyone that walks past it will see an empty house when in actual fact things have got out of control because there are three time dilators in the house, one working in the opposite direction to the other two and that has messed with it in all sorts of ways! If he hadn't put the filter on then we would have found them instantly. Not only that but it kept the implants from being scanned as well. I can't believe I didn't think of that!'

'Is that why when my mum came around she said she couldn't see anyone?' Sophie asked, glad that her mum wasn't going mad.

'Exactly,' Miss Sissins replied, 'Clara and her dads will be in there but you can only see her because you have seen through the perception filter. Now that you've broken it, everyone that walks past will be able to see what a state it's in.'

Miss Sissins was correct and Sophie immediately noticed an elderly couple who walked past the house and tutted at the state it had been left in.

Yasmine shrugged as if she wasn't really bothered what had caused the mess and started to fight her way through the undergrowth. It took them both a good five minutes to fight their way through the tall grass. There were large insects and bugs scattered through the grass, they also had clearly been affected by the time dilators. At one point, Yasmine screamed and sent a giant ant flying. As soon as it left the garden though, it returned to its regular size and scurried off across the pavement. When they did finally reach the house, Yasmine rubbed some of the dirt off the living room window.

'I can see her dads; look there they are, on the chairs,' Yasmine gestured for Sophie to come and see.

She had to look hard through the lace curtain that was draped across the window. (Sophie's Uncle Matthew had said it stopped the sunlight from beaming onto the TV). After allowing her eyes a few seconds to adjust, sure enough, there were her two uncles – Matthew and Josh – one sat on the settee and one in the arm chair like they were just going about ordinary business of watching television. They had the choice of watching on their implants but didn't like to be anti-social to Clara.

Without thinking, Yasmine tapped on the window; neither of them moved.

'Let's find the front door,' said Sophie, realising it wasn't going to be easy with all the grass, but, the two set off and eventually found it.

Yasmine tried the handle – it was locked.

'Do you think King has some kind of lock breaking equipment in the Shadow warehouse somewhere? We can do some fancy wizardry to open the lock, like you see in the films?'

Sophie just shook her head and asked Yasmine for a leg up. Once up, she started feeling around on top of the door frame. A split second later, armed with the key her uncles always hid up there, Sophie was back on the ground unlocking the door. Yasmine was clearly disappointed that she wasn't allowed to try out something new and exciting.

Slowly, Sophie pushed it open. The sound of the TV emanated from the living room – it must have been left switched on for the entire six weeks! Sophie had been told by Miss Sissins to not touch anything as it might have a bad effect on Clara's dads when they woke up. So, they ignored the sound and ventured upstairs to Clara's bedroom. The door was open so Sophie looked in and there she was, lying sideways on her bed with her hands under her head looking like she was just fast asleep in her school uniform. As Yasmine and Sophie got closer though, they could see that Clara wasn't right. Her face was pale and she had one of the time dilators attached to the side of her head. She had got marks where tears had rolled down her cheeks, over her nose and onto the bed. Sophie was shocked at what her cousin looked like. She had clearly been lying there since the last day of the last school year, which was when anyone that knew her had last seen her.

Remembering what Miss Sissins had told her, Sophie bent down so that her face was level with Clara's. She pushed the jet-black hair out of Clara's eyes and gently followed Miss Sissins's instructions about how to best peel off the time dilator. Sophie could feel the emotion building up inside of her. She had missed her cousin so much and now that she knew what she had been going through a huge rush of guilt flowed through her body. She wanted to be sick but couldn't, she wanted to cry but couldn't. She was feeling so many emotions all at once that she wished her mind would just pick one!

When Clara started waking up and rubbing her eyes, Sophie's mind decided on joy. She burst into a huge smile and, when she had had time to come to terms with where she was, Clara also smiled an enormous smile. The pair flung their arms around each other as Clara sat up. Yasmine sat on the bed next to Clara and the three girls all just hugged. None of them said anything; they just shared the grief and the sorrow that the last six weeks had brought. They had missed each other terribly but now they were back! Life was nowhere near the same but the three of them had each other and, for that short time, nothing else in the universe mattered.

After a minute or two, Clara just murmured through an onslaught of emotions, 'Thank you.

Chapter 20 – The Debrief

After the girls had just sat in silence for about a half an hour in Clara's room, the trio got comfortable and logged into their implants, they were under instruction from Miss Sissins to return to Shadow HQ for a debrief as soon as they had Clara but they took the opportunity to catch up first.

After a quick flash of lights, all three were stood in the main reception area of the building that the world was finding so reclusive; to Clara this place was nothing new but for Sophie and Yasmine there was a lot to take in.

The floor was a gleaming, shining white and around the edge of the room behind them stretched a huge, grey, U-shaped sofa with blue cushions. Behind that hung a piece of art that looked most unusual; it had a painting of a huge, gleaming white tower block that tickled the clouds and was surrounded by snow, which looked to be actually moving in the painting. All around the sky scraper, which reminded Sophie somewhat of somewhere but she couldn't pinpoint what, spacecraft hovered as if delivering or taking things away like lorries at a depot. Sophie studied it more carefully and could see tiny people drawn onto the painting – She could have sworn she saw them move as if they were almost waving at her. Her gaze didn't linger on it too long though as above them was a huge circular light. It dominated the ceiling and lit up the room like the sun itself. In front of the girls stood a long white reception desk, there was nothing on top of it and it gleamed like the floor. Behind the desk, on the wall, was written "Shadow" in amazing grey letters that curled round each other and to its right was a corridor that stretched for what looked like miles. This place was so clean and spotless that it had clearly remained untouched for a long time.

Knowing her way round already, Clara simply walked up to the desk and put her hand on the top of it. A light under her hand flashed red twice, then green. A few seconds later, footsteps could be heard coming, albeit slowly, down the corridor to the side of reception. Alton King appeared at the side of the desk.

'Clara Betts, welcome back,' King was still drained of emotion and even in this apparent relief, he seemed very robotic to Sophie.

'Did you not think to look for me at home?' Clara asked.

'Dale must have had some kind of perception filter on it. We scanned it with all the satellites but there was nothing there!' King now couldn't get his words out quickly enough; he was obviously incredibly relieved just to have her back. 'We need to give you the once over to make sure you're ok. You should be fine physically but, how long has it been for you?'

'Six months!' came Clara's reply.

'Six months!' King repeated, 'You've only been gone six weeks. I say only…'

Sophie could keep quiet no more as King gestured for them all to walk down the long corridor, 'You were in there for six months?' she exclaimed. The corridor was so long that Sophie and Yasmine couldn't see where it ended but they walked just the same, transfixed at the return of the friend who had vanished some six weeks ago.

'Yes, the time dilator was set to speed time up. So, six weeks for you was actually six months for me. Natan must have added in one of Miss Sissins's plugins – The Nightmare Program – so for the past six months I have been living my own worst nightmare,' Clara was being extremely open and blasé about what had happened. For someone trapped in their own worst nightmare for six months, she didn't seem massively affected.

'What did you see?' King asked, but Sophie had a suspicion that she knew the answer.

Clara explained that for six months she had been kept lying down in a tiny glass room. People in white coats would come and look at her and study her but she never saw any of their faces; they all wore masks – the kind that surgeons wear. Occasionally, she was allowed out but that was so she could be stood up and examined some more, she was unable to move her hands and feet of her own free will so escape was never an option. At this point Sophie realised that the second time she had seen Clara must have been at one of these moments. Clara also explained that a man kept coming to see her without a mask on - a man with spikey brown hair and kind but sad eyes. When he had visited, Clara had felt a lot safer but still had a strong desire to get out. Clara couldn't explain why this was her worst nightmare but she said she had never felt fear like it. Being out was clearly a huge relief to her and she was in no rush to talk about her nightmare further.

The corridor still showed no sign of finishing but King and Clara stopped. By now, they were all surrounded by almost pure white, on the walls, the floor and the ceiling, because the corridor was so long, even in front of them and behind them was nothing but sheer white. There was though a random line of black in the walls. King leant forward and ran his finger down it. The wall disappeared in front of them and revealed what appeared to be an examination room.

King turned to Sophie and Yasmine, 'You two wait here, I'm just going to examine Clara. We won't be five minutes.'

Clara nodded as if to reassure the other two. She clearly knew what she was doing and followed King into the room.

'How can you examine her?' Sophie asked, 'she's in her avatar?'

King smiled at the apparent ignorance of Sophie whereas Clara furrowed her brow, seemingly confused as to why her cousin didn't know the answer to that question.

'We can analyse her physical state through the avatar,' King replied and the pair disappeared as the wall reappeared again and Sophie and Yasmine were alone, together in the long white corridor. They simply sat on the floor and waited for the return of Clara and King.

They had barely sat down when they heard footsteps running up the corridor towards them. They wouldn't have been able to make out who it was had it not been for the fact that they only knew one other person ever came here – Miss Sissins. Eventually, as the footsteps got louder, her silhouette became clear and her short, dark hair became visible. She stopped at Yasmine and Sophie's feet and caught her breath. It was a good few seconds before she could get any words out, so Yasmine jumped in first.

'Are Clara's dads ok?'

'Yes,' replied Miss Sissins, still out of breath, 'they think there was a malfunction with their implant and that they were only there for six minutes. Can't wait to see what they say when they realise they were gone for six weeks!' Miss Sissins seemed remarkably excited by this so Sophie gave her a look.

'What will they do? What will they think Clara has been up to while they've been gone for six weeks?'

'It's ok; I told them she had been living with you and your parents. The truth will never get out.'

Miss Sissins wasn't sounding reassuring. At some point Amelia would talk to her brother about where he had been for six weeks, Clara would then come up in discussion and Miss Sissins's terrible idea would fall down.

'OK, I'll reprogram their implants and implant false memories.'

'You can do that!' Yasmine asked, aghast.

'Yazz, there isn't a lot I can't do with the freedom I have with these implants.'

'Yes, Clara said something about 'The Nightmare Program' that you invented,' Sophie said.

'Why would she mention that?' Miss Sissins asked and her face dropped.

'Apparently she's been in it for six months,' Yasmine replied.

Miss Sissins's face dropped further, 'She's what! Oh dear... err...' she paused for a moment, almost like the truth would be too much to handle at the moment, 'but this is the only solution for your uncles Soph,' she said, changing the subject, 'They will just think they have been away on holiday for six weeks. Anywhere they have ever talked about going to?'

Sophie was reluctant to accept Mr Sissins's idea but saw no other option, 'They always talked about New York,' she told her.

'New York it is then,' Miss Sissins flicked behind her ear again and changed into an old, rather large man with no hair.

He had a moustache and greasy skin that looked really disgusting. His clothes also changed into a blue shirt and trousers combination that accentuated his stomach and he had a name badge that read 'Mike'. Yasmine and Sophie stood there looking him up and down, they still hadn't gotten used to Miss Sissins changing right before their eyes; she noticed that they looked uneasy.

'This?' she said, pointing at her new face, 'he came to fix my electric meter once. Nice guy loved a doughnut or nine,'. At that, Miss Sissins disappeared again.

Sophie and Yasmine smiled at Miss Sissins's silly, randomness knowing she meant no harm and turned to where Clara and King had disappeared a few moments before. Sophie slumped down onto the floor again. She was mentally tired even if her avatar wasn't physically;

once again, the events of the week were catching up on her. She tried to put her head on Yasmine's shoulder and close her eyes but her head went straight through her. She could have slept just there and then in her school uniform even if she was an avatar. That was until Miss Sissins reappeared again as herself and the hole in the wall opened up at the same time.

Initially, Miss Sissins hadn't noticed the hole in the wall and started rambling again. 'Done, they spent a week stuck going up and down the Empire State Building because the lift had broken. Had the time of their li...' Miss Sissins noticed King with Clara stood next to him. Clara had a look on her face that showed both disgust and immense joy, all in one go.

Clara and Miss Sissins stared at each other, neither one wanting to be the first to speak.

Instead, Sophie did so, 'Clara, I...'

Clara shook her head but didn't say anything; she raised a finger to Sophie to prompt her to stop. Stepping forward tentatively, Clara began to walk towards Miss Sissins. She spoke slowly, as if very annoyed, as she did so.

'Do you know where I've been for six months?' she asked.

Miss Sissins shook her head.

'I've been in your Nightmare Program.'

At this, Miss Sissins's blank, sorrowful expression changed to one of concern and worry.

'I screamed and screamed for you to come and get me, but every message I sent bounced back. You send me in with only you as a contact, not even Mr King, and I can't contact you! What use is that?'

Miss Sissins looked at the floor again, 'You know I can't look at them,' she replied.

'This was life or death,' Clara replied straight away, 'you could have gotten me out after a day. You were my only hope. Months I spent trying to get through to you. But, you wouldn't look, not even when your only agent was in danger,' Clara's anger was rising now. Yasmine and Sophie had never seen her quite like this before.

'I can't open them Clara; you know why,' Miss Sissins sounded extremely apologetic but unwavering in her viewpoint.

Clara had got Miss Sissins on the ropes now. She was really suffering and was close to tears. She knew it was her fault; even though she and King knew it was the correct decision at the time, she couldn't bear the idea of people hating her for preserving the peace. Even when her closest ally was in clear danger, she simply couldn't face that much hatred. There would have been video messages, audio abuse and threats in a million other ways and Miss Sissins was too scarred by her actions to face the criticism yet. If she had a way to find them – fine – but there was no way that she knew of.

'That's enough, Clara,' King interrupted.

Clara could see she was upsetting Miss Sissins and so stood down. Miss Sissins looked at her very sorrowfully; she looked to have aged about ten years in the last two minutes.

'I'm sorry,' she mumbled, 'but you know I can't look at those messages. I sent those agents off into an unknown world with nothing, they despise me and it's because of my own stupidity. But I *was* right. I'd do it again in a heartbeat, but I would get the calculation right! This agency needs keeping secret, not people showing off in front of cameras, having worldly treasures given to them simply for doing their job. Shadow is the most important organisation in the world and I was right to do what I did.'

Miss Sissins's outburst seemed to change Clara's perspective slightly; she had spent six months away and was still in shock. She seemed to soften to what she had said, and looked remorseful for her explosion before. The two of them had shared some adventures recently and had formed a strong bond that had all started at school in year 5. Clara wasn't about to let that go. Miss Sissins was her teacher but was also now her friend and comrade when they were at Shadow and they needed each other's support not them falling out.

'How did you get a message to Sophie then if you couldn't message Mr King?' Yasmine asked, slightly confused.

'Being in there for six months and knowing what was going on, I was able to hack into the main server at Stratus, it seems to be pretty easy for me to connect to that place, and leave some clues for people. I tried to contact Sophie twice...'

Sophie nodded at this.

'...and I managed to leave some code for Mr King over there to use to track what I was doing. Between them, they managed to find me. All it needed was for you and Sophie to get your implant, which was easy as we had talked about it here before. I hear though that I did cause a bit of a problem with my second message to Sophie?'

'Yeah, the whole world fainted as you overloaded everyone's implant,' Yasmine added, helpfully.

'Ah, sorry,' was all Clara could say to that.

Sophie and Yasmine were now looking slightly bemused. They thought it had been Miss Sissins, King and Mr Houghton who had agreed they should get an implant. Now they were finding out that Clara had a say in it too. Clara noticed that Mr King and Miss Sissins also had guilty looks on their faces.

'Sophie and Yasmine have got access to all the right equipment, haven't they?' she asked, thinking she already knew the answer.

'Sort of,' Miss Sissins replied, 'they are still in soft-light though.'

'You two put my cousin and one of my best friends,'

'What do you mean "one of"?' Yasmine interrupted.

'Shut up, Yazz!' Clara said, 'you two put my cousin and my best friend through all this and you didn't give them a hard-light avatar!' Clara couldn't contain her shock. King and Miss Sissins had gone back to looking like they were being told off at school.

'Sophie, Yasmine, follow me. It's time you learn exactly what goes on here at Shadow.'

Clara then started walking down the corridor again. She looked like a girl on a mission. Sophie and Yasmine followed like excited sheep. The whole truth was finally about to come out.

Chapter 21 – Hard-Light

Clara continued her march down the pure white corridor, she was visibly excited at what she was about to show Sophie and Yasmine. The pair did their best to keep up but Clara seemed to have found an extra gear and was now motoring. After a few minutes, Clara stopped; she turned to talk to Sophie and Yasmine but had to wait for a second while they caught up and then caught their breath. Before she could speak though, her appearance seemed to change. Her hair went red and freckles appeared on her face. Clara quickly shook her head and her familiar face reappeared.

'What was that?' Sophie asked.

'My avatar appears to have glitched,' Clara replied, 'It's been like it since I was given it. Sometimes it changes my appearance without me asking it to. Miss Sissins has had a look and can't find what's causing it.'

'Are you ok with that?' Sophie asked.

'Doesn't matter too much, does it?' Clara asked.

'I suppose not,' Sophie replied, 'It might just take some getting used to if it happens a lot.'

'It only happens occasionally and even then, it's only for a few seconds,' Clara explained and Sophie decided that if it didn't bother Clara too much then it shouldn't bother her.

'I'm going to show you the three most important rooms and places we use at Shadow,' Clara began, dismissing Sophie's worry, 'The Playground – where, over time, we will hone your agent skills and turn you into the best, then there is Zatvor – which is not for the faint-hearted, apparently. I'm not sure. I've never seen it, only pictures and heard the stories. First time for everything though,' Clara was clearly getting excited at having someone to share all this with, 'First of all, though, here we are at the tech room or as Miss Sissins and I call it – The Shop Floor.'

Sophie and Yasmine were revitalised by the excitement. The tiredness they had felt previously was replaced with adrenaline. It was all a bit surreal, seeing one of their best friends show them around a part of her life that neither of them had any idea existed. It would be one thing if Clara had a hobby that neither of them knew about, but this was a whole new world that Yasmine and Sophie had no clue existed outside of Tom's stories.

Clara put her hand up against the wall and it flashed red then green as it had done in reception. Part of the wall separated and revealed an entrance to a room, much like the medical area that Clara had entered with King. Without a second thought, Clara walked in and Sophie and Yasmine followed. Once they had had the chance to take in their surroundings, Sophie and Yasmine noticed that they were in the same room as they were before, when they had first come to Shadow. Again, it was completely sparse. It was a plain, grey warehouse-type space with high walls and a long floor. There wasn't much to take in the first time never mind the second.

Clara continued to step forward for a few more paces then stopped.

'We've been here before,' Sophie said.

Clara turned her head slightly to let Sophie know she had heard her but then muttered, 'not like this you haven't.'

Clara clicked her fingers. She turned around showing a huge smile of pride and excitement on her face. Sophie and Yasmine looked at her as if waiting for her to do something else; they weren't waiting long.

Underneath their feet, the room began to shake. It was like a giant earthquake. Sophie went to grip Yasmine's shoulder to keep her balance but, because they were in their avatars and were still just projections of themselves, her hand went straight through her; she almost fell to the floor. Clara stood there – grinning, completely relaxed. The shaking got more and more violent until things started emerging from the floor. All around the room, pillars of white started to grow. Some rose to knee height, others rose to eye level. The tops of them were about the size of a dinner plate. It was as if a white forest was growing within the huge room and it wasn't stopping. More and more pillars started sprouting from the floor. Some were now growing as high as the ceiling and still they kept emerging from the floor. However, through the room there was a path where nothing had grown; this appeared, to Sophie, to allow people to walk in amongst the strange white towers. As the shaking finished, Sophie and Yasmine straightened themselves up. The growths had stopped and so had the shaking. Clara clicked her fingers again and all of the tops of the cylindrical tubes flipped over. There was now some sort of object on top of each one or, if there wasn't an object, a green light emanating upwards from the top of the tube, each with a card that had a name on it. Sophie noticed that the car from last time was still there but this time it was on the other side of the warehouse and was completely swamped by a million other objects.

'Come on,' Clara beckoned.

The girls followed behind her as Clara continued her exposition of what exactly was going on.

'This is every piece of tech that Mr King and Miss Sissins have invented in the last few years. Some are copies of things they made before The Departure that have been reworked, others are brand new. Everything is top secret and definitely not to be made available to anyone outside of this room, for now.'

Sophie stared at everything she could and tried to read as many labels as possible. She caught a glimpse of one of the tubes with a green light and read the card.

'Heat Vision Plugin – allows the user to see the world through a heat-sensitive camera to detect body heat.'

Sophie had no time to ask Clara questions as she was hurrying off into the distance again, weaving in and out of the white towers, following the path to a destination unknown. Sophie caught sight of another tube; this one appeared to have a brown satchel on the top.

'B.P. Bag – allows the wearer to carry an infinite amount of equipment so that they always have what they need.'

Next to that was a photo frame with a picture in which the people seemed to be animated and waving. It read, 'DigiPhoto - a clever way to store data to avoid it being stolen.'

Sophie's attention was then caught by inventions like 'The Food Copier – creates food for anyone, anywhere' and 'The H2O Creator – will give the owner water whenever they desire'. It was these that made her think back to what Mr Houghton or Dale Natan had said about there being inventions in Shadow, which King had chosen not to use, that could change the world for the better.

The trio kept on walking. Sophie and Yasmine both read various other labels. Eventually, Clara stopped. She turned, took a ball out of her pocket and threw it to Yasmine. Yasmine reacted quickly and would have caught it, however, it travelled straight through her hand and onto the floor behind her.

'How come you can throw that ball and open that door?' Sophie asked, remembering that her cousin was an avatar as well yet she was able to do everyday tasks that she and Yasmine couldn't, 'If we are all projected here with light, which we are as we are actually all back in your room, then you should go through everything as well.'

Clara didn't say anything; she simply put her hand on top of one of the tubes with a green light emanating from it. Sophie leaned forward, and it read…

'Hard-Light – Allows the user to be a physical presence when logged in as an Internet Implant user.'

In the corner of Sophie's eye, a familiar red dot began to flash. Knowing exactly what to do this time, Sophie stared at the empty space in front of the objects before her.

'You have one new plugin waiting to be installed,' it read when Sophie zoned in.

She then heard Clara's voice, 'Install it,' she instructed, 'then you should be able to touch things in the same way I can.'

Sophie clicked on the link and instantaneously a download bar appeared but promptly disappeared again. Sophie zoned back into the room.

Ready and waiting was Clara, she threw the ball to Yasmine again who this time caught it.

'Woah!' Yasmine mimed, excited.

'We can touch while being an avatar?' Sophie asked.

Clara simply nodded, 'One of Mr King's most important inventions. It's changed the way we go about things completely. Now that we can project ourselves somewhere and touch whilst there, it's literally like being in two places at once. However, remember, we are zoned out in one of those places,' Clara added, seemingly shooting her own argument down.

Yasmine threw the ball to Sophie who caught it and threw it back to Clara.

'What else have you got?' Yasmine asked, almost rudely, expecting to be given something else. Sophie though was still taking in this new ability to touch. She wandered over to one of the white towers and put her hand on it. It was so soft, like touching cotton wool. She stroked it for a few seconds before something caught her eye. To her left, at about eye level, was a tube that had nothing on it. No object, no light, nothing, except for a card that only had two words written on it – 'Time Travel.'

'What's this one?' Sophie asked.

Clara came and stood behind her, looking over her shoulder, Yasmine stood over her other shoulder.

'That's the big one. If Mr King could only invent one more thing for the rest of his life it would be time travel. We already sort of go forwards in time with a sped-up dilator but that just gives an impression of what the future might look like, it's not an accurate prediction. Many years ago, he did experiment with sending someone forwards by 30 seconds but that agent was never seen again. Mr King wants to make it a reality that we can go back and forth in time. He knows he will be able to do it, just not yet.'

Sophie thought about that last part of the sentence for a few seconds before dismissing it as an interesting choice of phrase by Clara.

'Alright, next,' Clara began, 'I need to show you how you're going to be trained.'

'No more plugins or apps?' Yasmine sounded disappointed.

'Not yet, plenty of time for that, you already have everything I've got,' Clara replied, trying to soften Yasmine's disappointment.

Clara clicked her fingers again and all the tubes lowered themselves back into the floor. There was distinctly less shaking this time and the girls made their way back out of the warehouse and back into the white corridor. Yasmine took great satisfaction in putting her hand up next to the door and watching it go red and then green.

'Check you out, you're a natural,' Clara said in what Sophie knew as her sarcastic, patronising but harmless way.

Yasmine turned her nose up and the three friends set off on the next part of their enlightenment.

Chapter 22 – Agents in Training

A few more steps down the white corridor, Clara stopped again; this time in front of a monitor that seemed to be randomly placed on the wall. It was black at first but, as Clara lifted her hand to it, a few lights began to flicker and words appeared that Sophie couldn't quite make out. Clara busily pressed buttons on a touchpad under the monitor; words flashed up on the screen at some speed. Sophie had seen her at school, typing on a laptop (something adults no longer needed) and she had never been that quick. After a few seconds, Clara finished what she was doing and turned to look at the pair of them.

'Ready?' she asked as if Sophie and Yasmine were expected to know what she was talking about.

'For what?' Yasmine asked.

'This is 'The Playground'. It's where all the agents that have ever worked here were trained both mentally and physically. It contains computer-generated copies of levels from every computer game, film, myth, legend, television program, historical battle and book that Mr King and Miss Sissins could program. Each of them presents its own unique challenge and tests the agent in different ways to make sure they are made of 'the right stuff'. Clara was turning into quite the tour guide.

'So, it's a test?' Sophie asked, astutely.

'Sort of,' replied Clara, 'more of a training exercise.'

'So, what do we do?' Yasmine always liked the idea of a challenge and seemed excited.

'Well, we pick an exercise, I explain what you have to do and in you go. Finish the objective and you move on to another one which will help to improve you as agents. Do you want to have a go?' Clara made it all sound so simple.

'What do *you* think we should do?' Sophie turned the tables quite quickly on Clara and put the focus back on her.

'I think I know just the one to start you off,' Clara set about typing on the pad again and after a few presses, she was ready. 'Now don't worry, you can't get hurt.'

All of a sudden, the smile was wiped off Yasmine's face, she had no intention of even thinking about getting hurt. Now, she was wondering what exactly was behind the door.

'This is 'The Asterion Labyrinth'. It will test your physical speed, thinking skills, problem-solving and survival. It will try and play tricks on your mind, but just remember none of it is real; it's just like a computer game. Got it?'

Sophie and Yasmine both nodded.

'Think so,' said Yasmine, not quite as sure as she had been.

'So, what is our objective?' Sophie asked.

'Just survive in there for three minutes,' Clara smiled.

'Survive?' Before Yasmine could worry anymore, Clara opened the door and pushed them both in.

'Oh, and nobody has ever managed to finish this level on their first attempt!' Clara said as the door shut.

Sophie and Yasmine found themselves in a narrow alley. On both sides of them, about ten feet tall, were solid grey bricks, which were completely smooth; any thought of trying to climb them would be pointless. In front of them, stretched out for about 100 metres, was a floor of a brown, clay-like substance. Yasmine turned around to look for the door that Clara had pushed them through; it had disappeared and been replaced by another 100 metres of brown clay and ten-foot-high walls going in the opposite direction. Yasmine was about to say something to Sophie when they heard a noise – it wasn't one either of them liked the sound of - a huge banging sound, like metal on stone. Sophie noticed that the walls shook as the sound reverberated around them and surmised that something had hit the wall with an immense force. Sophie stood stock still and didn't flinch. Yasmine looked decidedly more nervous. The vibrating of the walls stopped and was replaced by something new. CLOMP, CLOMP: footsteps, loud, heavy footsteps. For something to make a noise like that on a clay floor it must have been huge. Along with the footsteps was another noise, a kind of grating sound, like something being dragged along the floor. Taking all this in, Sophie turned to Yasmine.

'Asterion, I know that word!' Sophie said in realisation.

Yasmine looked to her left in thought.

'I remember my dad using it before in one of his stories.'

Sophie looked back to Yasmine wearing the look of someone who had suddenly worked out an answer that they really didn't want to know. 'Asterion was the real name of the creature that lived in the Labyrinth. It wreaked havoc in Greece, killed hundreds, if not thousands, of people that it found had wandered into its maze.'

'With the body of a man and head of a bull?' said Yasmine, now realising what Sophie was going to say and remembering one of the myths that her dad *had* shared with her.

'The Minotaur.'

The grating got louder, as did the footsteps. They were getting closer, almost directly in front of the pair of them now. BANG! The walls vibrated again, and this time the ground shook violently.

From a gap in the wall, about twenty metres in front of them, a figure began to emerge. It must have been ten feet tall, like the walls. The first thing to appear from around the corner was the horns, which rose higher than the walls themselves, they were long and piercing, but battle-worn, these horns had done some damage in the past and were looking to do some more. Then came the nose. Through the middle of it was a huge silver ring. Droplets of blood spread around it. From its mouth hung drool; this beast was hungry and the slobber dangled from its lips like honey from a beehive. Most striking though were the red eyes. Like balls of flailing fire, they instantaneously saw Sophie and Yasmine and latched onto them. The Minotaur had their scent.

Sophie and Yasmine continued to edge backwards away from the monster but they were hypnotised by the brute in front of them. The rest of the bull appeared. He was wearing armour over one shoulder and padding across his human shins. Behind him, he dragged the source of the scraping noise – his axe. The blade alone was the size of Sophie and the handle it was attached to was the height of her and Yasmine on each other's shoulders.

Now in full view, the Minotaur stopped in the centre of the alley and glared at the two aliens who had dared enter his labyrinth. Raising the axe above his head, he let out the most ear-shattering roar the girls had ever heard. As he did so, he brought the axe down and swept it to the side into the wall to send another thunderous, threatening message to Sophie and Yasmine.

The girls didn't need telling again. They turned the opposite way and ran for their lives!

Finding a gap in the wall, Sophie and Yasmine turned sharply right and paused to catch their breath. Behind them, the noise had faded slightly as the Minotaur hadn't kept pace with the girls but it began to gradually grow louder again.

Struggling for breath, Yasmine stuttered, 'Who defeated the Minotaur?'

'It was Theseus in the myth, who knows which agent from Shadow it was in reality!' Sophie replied, thinking back to what her dad had told her, 'but he had the sword of Aegeus and I can't see it lying around, can you?'

'OK, so if we can't defeat it then we have to get out,' Yasmine exclaimed.

'No, Clara said the task was to survive for three minutes, not to find a way out of here or defeat it. The Minotaur hunting us is the challenge, not the idea that we have to defeat it.'

Perversely, Sophie was enjoying herself; the contest had been set and she was applying logic to everything she had seen and heard. All those years of reading and listening to her dad were paying off.

The thud of the Minotaur's steps was getting louder and louder, closer and closer. He let out another booming roar and thumped his axe against the brick walls. Sophie closed her eyes and tried to think - hard.

'We have to keep running,' Yasmine said, having caught her breath.

'Agreed, let's find another turning,' Sophie turned and darted away from the oncoming destruction that was the Minotaur.

As soon as the girls started running again, Sophie noticed that the Minotaur's footsteps quickened as well. The thuds got a lot closer together and the dragging sound sped up as well. An idea popped into Sophie's head, she slowed down in an effort to test her theory.

'What are you doing?' Yasmine turned around and shouted at Sophie.

'Trust me,' Sophie replied. She was sounding more and more like Clara had done since they found her.

As Sophie predicted, the Minotaur's footsteps slowed down as well. Sophie decided to completely stop. The Minotaur slowed down again but didn't stop completely as Sophie had. The thunderous steps were now the same pace as when they had started. Also slowing right down, Yasmine had noticed the same thing that Sophie had. Sophie nodded at Yasmine to show that they were both thinking the same thing.

'So, what happens if we walk towards it?' Sophie asked.

'Do we really want to find out?' Yasmine replied.

'Clara said it would test our thinking skills and problem-solving. Running away just makes it run faster, stopping makes it slow down. We can't keep running full pelt for three minutes, it'll catch us because it's so much faster than us. We need to think differently. We need to go towards it. It's only a game, it can't hurt us.'

Yasmine could think of nothing else to contradict Sophie and so reluctantly agreed with her. Together the pair turned to face the demon. The turning they had come down was about ten metres behind them; they both started to slowly walk towards it. As they walked, the soft sound of the clay beneath their feet became much more pronounced. Sophie listened for the Minotaur, the footsteps had ceased, as had the dragging. What the girls could hear now was the deep breathing of the huge brute. In a way, it scared them more than the footsteps and the dragging because now they were moving towards it. At least it felt right running away from it. Sophie and Yasmine knew that in just a few seconds they would be mere metres away from their hunter.

'What if we just slow right down and barely move, but do actually keep moving?' Yasmine asked. Sophie shrugged and stood still, shuffling her feet ever so slightly in the direction of the turning. From around the corner, the Minotaur picked up one of his feet slowly and placed it down, very slightly in front of the other.

'He's still coming,' Sophie realised, 'we have to keep moving, properly.'

Eventually, the girls reached the final turning. With a huge amount of trepidation, Sophie walked cautiously around it. Stood about three metres in front of her was the Minotaur. It was so close that Sophie could smell the incredible stink that emanated from him. It smelt disgusting, flies hovered around his face and he just stared ahead beyond Sophie and Yasmine. Still edging forwards, Sophie took in the greasy hair and muscular build. This truly was an enormous creature. Sophie could almost reach out and touch him now, but still, she crept closer. Yasmine was slightly further behind but again still moving. The Minotaur did not react to their presence; he simply stared forwards above Sophie and Yasmine's heads, apparently oblivious to anything going on around him. He was the keeper of the labyrinth and nothing was going to get away from him. Sophie could now feel the heat coming off him, it warmed her face but the stench was foul and overpowering.

Thoughts flooded Sophie's mind. This was what she wanted from her life - to experience the mythical creatures that the adults had forgotten. This was so much more than she could imagine. The idea of what her dad would say if he knew what she was doing made her smile. Every other person on the planet was wasting away, staring at a screen and here was Sophie experiencing something amazing like this! The rest of the world was welcome to their pointless existences as far as Sophie was concerned.

If Sophie had the chance at that exact moment, she would have complimented King on exactly how well he had coded the game; it truly was like facing the real thing. Reaching the point whereby if she moved again she would be moving past the Minotaur and therefore away from it again, Sophie didn't know what to do. Her only option was to touch his hand. She very slowly reached out her hand towards his. Nerves were beginning to take hold of her; she was shaking almost uncontrollably and her breathing stopped as she took one sharp breath in. She took his immense hand and could feel the blood pumping through him. At that point, the Minotaur looked down at her. There was a new softness in his eyes. Sophie relaxed and breathed out. Half a second later though and the Minotaur had picked up his axe and brought it down on Sophie. The previously bricked-up walls and clay floor had turned to black and a door appeared behind Sophie and Yasmine. It flung open and in it stood Clara.

'You were so close! I didn't get anywhere near that close on my first attempt,' she screeched excitedly.

Sophie and Yasmine looked baffled. 'How long did we last?' Yasmine asked.

'Well over two minutes! You realised very quickly things that Mr King says lots of people miss. Loads of adults just run away and try to keep going for three minutes; he always catches them. You spotted that you had to go close to him. Just wait until Mr King sees this. You really are going to make excellent additions to the Shadow team.'

Sophie and Yasmine were still out of breath from their experience and so didn't say half the things they wanted to. Clara did point out that because they were in their avatars, the sensation of being out of breath wasn't actually real and was just a natural reaction. Neither Sophie nor Yasmine felt particularly helped by that remark.

'I've already seen it Clara; very impressive Sophie and Yasmine,' came a voice from down the corridor.

Sophie and Yasmine stepped through the doors out of The Playground and saw Miss Sissins coming towards them.

'I knew this was the right decision. I've said it for a long time now. We don't need adult agents, especially those who want glory and praise. Children are where the future is!'

Yasmine and Sophie were practically beaming now that they had caught their breath and heard such amazing praise from one of the people who had devised everything around them.

'Where are we going now, Clara?' Yasmine asked excitedly.

'Can't we have another go in there, on a different game?' Sophie also chimed in.

'No,' said Miss Sissins, rather sternly, 'now it is time for you to go home. Yasmine, your dad is due back from work in a few minutes and Sophie, your mum and dad will be wondering where you are if you don't get home soon.'

The three girls all looked rather disappointed. They had had such an amazing time since they had turned up at Clara's house to find her. Their lives had changed so much and they had seen a side of the world that not many people got to see. The comedown of having to go home and do normal things was going to be hard.

'All this will be here when you come back. It isn't going anywhere,' Miss Sissins did her best to reassure them, but their excitement and enthusiasm were at fever pitch, the three of them working together saving the world from anything that came their way. *Bring it on*, Sophie thought to herself.

Eventually, the girls admitted that enough was enough and that they still had a responsibility to their parents as well. The three zoned back into Clara's bedroom, which they had left some three hours before. Clara walked them downstairs and opened the front door. The three hugged and said 'goodbye' to each other. It felt so good for Sophie to have her cousin back in her life. She had missed her tremendously and to not just have her back, but to have her back like this, was greater than Sophie could have possibly imagined.

'Thank you, again,' said Clara as they said goodbye.

'That's what we're here for,' Yasmine replied.

'Wasn't there something else you wanted to show us?' Sophie remembered.

'Yeah, Zatvor,' Clara replied, 'but believe me, that's best saved for another day. Say hi to your mum and dad for me and I'm guessing my dads will be in touch with her soon!'

'Will do!' Sophie hugged her cousin again.

In the front garden, Clara's dads were busy tidying up what had become of their lawn. The tall grass had been just about trimmed back and the place was beginning to look back to normal. Clara spotted them, sprinted out into the garden and hugged them both. Sophie waved to her uncles and set off on the journey home. It had been a very eventful day!

Sophie raced back home and burst in the door. The first thing she wanted was her mum and dad. She found them both in the kitchen getting tea ready. She threw her arms around them. They didn't quite know what to say, so didn't say anything and made the most of having the affection.

'Tea in ten minutes,' dad said.

'Clara says hi,' Sophie replied.

Amelia and Tom looked at each other as Sophie left the room. Amelia followed and told Tom to stir the beans. She shouted after Sophie but she didn't listen. So, Amelia just sat on the settee and zoned out.

Whilst eating tea, Sophie noticed the flashing red light in the corner of her eye meaning she had a message waiting. Not ready to reveal to her parents that she had an implant, she finished her tea, thanked her parents and scurried off to her room. Her mum and dad were so distracted by the jolly, happy girl who ate with them that they were oblivious to anything being amiss.

'Where are you going?' Tom asked.

'Homework,' Sophie shouted whilst walking into her room, 'don't disturb me.'

Amelia and Tom just smiled to themselves; it was great to see their girl smiling again.

Once in her room, Sophie shut the door behind her and lay on her bed. She stared at the space just in front of her and the words 'One message received' became clear on a white screen. Sophie clicked on it and read the message.

'Sophie,

Ask King where the agents _really_ are.

The message remained unsigned and there was no name in the sent box but Sophie suspected she knew who it had come from. She forwarded it to King, Clara and Yasmine who messaged back almost immediately with the same thing – Mr Houghton or Dale Natan. They were going to need a chat with their head teacher and the sooner the better.

Chapter 23 – Not as Wrong as They Thought

It was Friday morning. Sophie, Yasmine and Clara all met up early outside Sophie's flat. Together, with the help of Miss Sissins, they were going to give Mr Houghton the grilling of a lifetime. Trying to provoke them into questioning King like that was a step too far in Clara's eyes. King had looked after her while she had been in training and she wasn't going to let anyone bad mouth or try and start rumours about him. The girls walked to school with a spring in their step; Yasmine and Sophie had had their lives flipped upside down and were both brimming with confidence. Clara walked more with an air of determination; she was back and looked all set to turn school on its head.

The sun had risen and was shining down on the trio as they made their way to school for an early start. They had arranged to meet Miss Sissins at school early so that they could get to Mr Houghton before school started to avoid a scene.

Nerves started to run through Sophie as they rounded the corner to school and the hedgerow around the field where it all started came into view. Unlike Tuesday, it was empty today. The silence of the village resonated with the girls and they took a deep breath as they continued their journey around the edge and set off up the drive.

'Ready?' Clara asked.

'Of course,' Yasmine replied, all ready to go storming into school.

Before she could set off though, Sophie heard someone shouting her name from behind her. She turned and noticed a figure running towards them wearing the lavender school uniform. The voice repeated its shout and it became clear that running towards them was Katie. As she got closer, Sophie noticed that her hair was a mess, her uniform was in a state and she looked exhausted.

'Sophie, I have to talk to you,' Katie staggered.

'We can't right now,' Yasmine replied.

Katie looked slowly at Clara and gave her an evil stare. This upset Sophie because Clara and Katie had been really good friends before Clara disappeared. Katie's feeling that Clara was yet another person who had abandoned her was too much to get over just yet. Of course, Clara would be unable to tell Katie the truth so they were caught between a rock and a hard place for now.

'But this can't wait; I have to tell you something,' Katie was beginning to panic.

Sophie was torn, yes Katie was quiet and slightly odd but she had never made a scene like this. She must have had something vital to say but right now there was the threat of the Earth being sent into chaos by vengeful mythical creatures and aliens who were about to invade the planet. Katie would *have* to wait as much as it upset Sophie.

'Find us at break time,' Sophie said, trying desperately to calm her friend.

'But…' Katie started to argue but then looked at the three girls and saw that there was no way she was going to change their minds.

'Oh, forget it then, I tried,' Katie huffed and stormed off in the opposite direction, away from school.

'What do you think she wanted?' Sophie asked nobody in particular.

'Probably something about her mum and how unhappy she is, nothing that can't wait until break time,' Yasmine said, shrugging off Katie's desperation, whereas Sophie furrowed her brow; she wasn't convinced that was it.

'Come on,' said Clara, who had moved on towards the school driveway.

In the car park, the three of them caught sight of Miss Sissins. She stood there in one of her blouses and black trousers. The sun shone on her glasses meaning that at first, they couldn't see her eyes. As the three got closer, they could see that she had the same look of determination in her eyes that they had. Respect came over the three of them again, seeing Miss Sissins as their teacher seemed to feel completely different to seeing Miss Sissins as the Shadow agent. Clara felt less like the boss in this environment and so Miss Sissins led the discussion.

'What's all this about then, girls? Mr King told me to meet you here before school.'

'If you'd open your messages you'd know,' said Clara, straight away, her respect failing.

Miss Sissins pointed at her and warned her to watch it as they were at school now. Sophie looked around the car park again and spotted Mr Houghton's car. He was here already. The only other person around was Mrs Tabard and she was in the canteen cooking the dinners so she wouldn't be a distraction. This was their moment.

With Miss Sissins leading the way, the three girls followed her into school and marched down the corridor towards Mr Houghton's office. Excited at the prospect of dramatically knocking on the door and swinging it open in a display of power, Clara was disappointed when, a few metres away from the door, Mr Houghton came out of his office and gestured for them all to come in. It caught them off guard; clearly, Mr Houghton had been expecting them and this seemed to be all part of his plan.

Without saying a word between them, the three girls and Miss Sissins sat themselves down in Mr Houghton's office. Closing the door behind them, Mr Houghton sat on his taller chair to give himself an even stronger sense of power and control.

'Hello Clara, welcome back,' Mr Houghton talked with a sense of ownership as though everything was going the way he wanted it to.

Clara didn't reply and just glared at him.

'OK, not in a talkative mood, neither would anyone be after six months of...' Mr Houghton stopped himself mid-sentence and decided not to finish it as Clara knew exactly what he was talking about. Clara shuffled in her chair, Mr Houghton was getting to her but she was doing incredibly well to hide it.

'Where are my agents then?' Mr Houghton asked with a sense of sincerity in his voice, like he actually cared and didn't genuinely know where any of them were, 'I take it you have asked King and he has told you to come and let me know.'

Yasmine was the first to bite, 'Why don't you know? I... sorry... we, don't know, they were uploaded by Miss Sissins in The Departure but lost somewhere.'

Miss Sissins bowed her head. It never got any easier to hear how it was her mistake that all the agents had been lost; hearing a child and this child in particular say it was somehow even worse.

Sophie was still baffled. To the best of her knowledge, the agents had been uploaded as part of The Departure and nobody had any idea where they were. Why was there even a discussion about somebody knowing where they were?

Mr Houghton tutted and smiled to himself. He then shook his head as if he was being told something he already knew not to be true, 'Think this through Yasmine, why would I know where they are? If I knew where they were, I would find them, get them out and I'd be setting up an agency of my own. *I* haven't hidden them away or ruined their lives; they could be of massive use to me. Sissins, you have a stronger interest than most in finding them, isn't your...' Mr Houghton was cut off by Miss Sissins partway through.

'Don't you say another word!' Miss Sissins was angry and she slammed her hands down on the arms of the chair.

'Have they not messaged you? Not even your... you know who?' Mr Houghton was toying with Miss Sissins. He had found a way to make her angry and that gave Mr Houghton the upper hand.

'I can't look!' Miss Sissins interrupted with a mumbled response.

Mr Houghton laughed at this and simply asked.

'Why not? If I'm right then they won't hate you. They'd be calling out for help. If Clara can find a way to hack into the system to get a message to Sophie then who knows, they might have found a way to relay where they are.'

'Open your messages,' Sophie said without thinking it through any more than she needed to. Everything that Mr Houghton was saying was correct. It was time for Miss Sissins to see if any of them had managed to relay their position to her.

Miss Sissins looked at her with resignation on her face, as if she already knew that she had to do it.

'If they are all abusive and horrible, then you can shut them down straight away. If though, Mr Houghton is right, then there might well be a lot of people who we can help,' Sophie said as sincerely as she could, seeing that her teacher was struggling.

Miss Sissins shook nervously but nodded reluctantly. The thoughts that had been weighing her down since her darkest day all those years ago were about to be either lifted or pushed down even harder. She had spent years thinking she had lost the lives of all those people who wanted no more than to receive some credit. For years, she was convinced that she had done the right thing but within the last few minutes, Mr Houghton had made her doubt herself and manipulate her into doing the one thing she swore she would never do. She couldn't think about it any longer and zoned out in front of everyone to check her messages.

Clara gasped as she did so. She had most definitely not expected her to do it. She knew exactly how tough this was going to be for her.

Opening her message folder, Miss Sissins was met with a blank screen which simply read 'NO NEW MESSAGES'. *That's odd*, she thought to herself. But then, the screen started to light up as the messages flooded through. Within about a second, the display had changed to 11,000 and kept climbing. Miss Sissins paused the arrival of messages and scrolled through them. They were all names she recognised. As she scrolled through the content of the messages, it became obvious that they had been doctored and edited so that they couldn't be read. Message after message was blacked out. Someone had tampered with them so that even if Miss Sissins were to open her messages, she wouldn't know what to do with them as she couldn't read them.

Eventually, she found one that was so short it either hadn't been noticed or the corruptor assumed it didn't have anything that needed censoring – Samantha Robertson – a top agent who had saved the world many times and one of her closest friends. The subject of the message read 'HELP!'

Don't trust King. Art. Get us out!

She un-paused the arrival of new ones and allowed all of them to flow through. Eventually, the final figure ended up at 20,683. They all said the same thing. They needed help and they needed it soon but she couldn't tell where they were. All the messages were blanked out except that one. Checking the date on the first messages, they were all from about ten years ago. She checked the dates on the most recent ones. They had become a lot fewer and further between as agents had given up hope of being rescued. One name though kept appearing more than any other – Cole – Miss Sissins weighed it up but decided she couldn't bring herself to read any of his right now – it would simply be too difficult. *Later on,* she thought to herself and zoned back into Mr Houghton's office.

'I'm right, aren't I?' Mr Houghton said smugly, rocking back on his chair, 'They all know where they are.'

Miss Sissins nodded, 'But they have been edited and blacked out so that I can't read them,' she then forwarded the one from Samantha that remained unedited to the imposing head teacher.

'King,' Mr Houghton said, 'he knows where they are.'

'Girls, we have to go to Shadow, right now,' Miss Sissins said without flinching.

Seeing how straight-faced and shaken Miss Sissins was, the girls all agreed, then and there, that it was the right thing to do.

'And I'm coming too,' Mr Houghton said, confidently.

Clara couldn't quite believe what she heard and scoffed at Mr Houghton's idea. Miss Sissins looked at Clara to reassure her and nodded in agreement with her nemesis.

'You aren't serious?' Clara screeched, in a state of disbelief.

'He was right, Clara. Mr King has their consciences locked up somewhere at Shadow. The messages show that. Mr Natan has earned the right to come with us. He will only be zoning in any way. There is too much at stake for him to try anything.'

Clara pursed her lips and shook her head before she zoned out. Yasmine and Miss Sissins followed, leaving Sophie and Mr Houghton as the last ones. Sophie looked at Mr Houghton before she zoned out. He was smirking on one side of his face; his eyes lit up, like the time Sophie had left his office when he had asked about Clara. Sophie knew he wasn't playing an honest game but she couldn't prove otherwise. She had to go along with it; she didn't trust Mr Houghton at all, now that she had seen him with *that* look. A few minutes ago, she had been questioning Mr King's trustworthiness; now, she was leaning the other way. To say that she was torn between who to follow and who to have faith in, would be an understatement. Before zoning out, she took one last glance around Mr Houghton's office. The last thing she saw was the photo on his desk of him with his wife and son.

Chapter 24 – Fox in the Hen House

King was in his office doing nothing in particular. With his implant, he had no use for computers and with nobody being allowed into Shadow, he had no use for visitors and therefore cleaners. As a result, his existence was lonely but he was content, he had spent years protecting what was most dear to him – the privacy of his own life and that of his company that he had built from the ground up from a very young age.

Moping around his office, the events of the last few days had made him contemplate what he might try and invent next; the thing that had bugged him the most was travel through time and space. Space he decided could be doable, if he had knowledge of any places in particular he could simply zone out there, but he didn't and even then, he doubted whether the signal required to run an avatar would stretch very far into space. Over the years his agents had caught many aliens and creatures from other worlds but none of them were willing to share anything with the man who had brought about their capture. They did speak almost universally about one creature that travelled from planet to planet with an army all of their own, much in the way that King himself dreamt of but he never got much information from them other than they should be all scared of this "Crusader" as they called themselves and how they had shaped worlds to befit what they saw as perfect. King was scared of this being who, as far as he knew, only went by one name - Condenar. The tales that aliens told described someone who would take over the world and ruin what King had turned it into. This frightened him because all he ever wished for was his company to live on long after he was gone and if this Crusader made it to Earth then it might take that away.

So, for now, space was out. Time was another issue completely; travelling forward he couldn't see as a problem, he just needed to find a way that didn't make an agent disappear forever in front of his eyes. It was travelling backwards that he couldn't see possible. It was no good sending agents to the future if you couldn't bring them back! Also, even going back in time 5 minutes would cause massive issues as there would be two of you in one place and this would automatically change events even if you didn't want to. However, having invented almost everything else he could think of, this was what kept him awake at night; that and the fear of someone finding the agents that he locked away years ago and blamed on Jane.

With the thought of them being discovered now being more likely than it had been in the last ten years racing through his brain, he had come to the realisation that his time might be up. It was time to leave his agency in the hands of children. Not as many children as he would have liked but the three girls had proven themselves capable nonetheless. There was still the niggling doubt that if they failed and his company's secrets were let out then he would have to step back in but that was a risk that he had control over. The return of the agents was the greater of the two evils so the children it would have to be.

A light started flashing in the corner of his eye. He zoned out and looked at it; there had been a security breech on The Shop Floor. Someone who wasn't supposed to be there was inside. He knew who it was; only one person knew how to get in to that exact place and would even know that place existed who wasn't Jane Sissins.

Knowing Dale Natan had returned to Shadow, King activated the safety protocol he had put in place years ago to allow for such a scenario, he smiled sadly and saw this as the huge opportunity he had been waiting for. He zoned back in again and made his way out of the office, before turning back to look at the place he had called home for ten years one last time.

On the Shop Floor, Sophie, Yasmine, Clara, Miss Sissins and Mr Houghton, now in his avatar, which looked like Dale Natan, were stood in the completely empty warehouse. Natan tried to click his fingers to release the inventions but it didn't do anything. He looked at his hand, baffled. It used to work when he worked there.

'It's not your hand, is it,' Miss Sissins said, 'that's not your real body so it won't recognise your click. And anyway, don't you think Mr King would have taken away all your privileges?'

Natan tutted and grunted to himself and began to get restless very quickly, 'Where is he?' he moaned.

'Oh, stop whining,' Clara began, 'he'll be here, then we can put an end to this rubbish. As if Mr King has kept backups of all the agents locked away in here for ten years and not told anyone about it!'

Sophie twitched slightly as to her Clara was wrong. To her King *had* hidden them away. That's where all the evidence was pointing anyway. Sophie could see that he was a man obsessed with things like protecting the privacy and integrity of his company over the lives of millions of mythicals, so hiding away agents and letting Miss Sissins accept the guilt sounded like something he would definitely do.

Sophie and Yasmine looked around; the room was identical to when they had first arrived at Shadow earlier in the week. Nothing was on display, just huge grey walls with nothing on them. At the end of the room, the large door began to creak open. Sophie squinted to try and make out who it was; it didn't take much guessing. Walking towards them, with his hands behind his back, was King. He took an age to get to the middle of the warehouse where all the others stood.

The clonking footsteps echoed around the room as no other sound dared to interrupt the great man as he walked.

King did eventually reach a close enough distance to the others, Natan was getting more animated, but Clara spoke first.

'Mr King, please can you clear this up. He…' Clara pointed at Natan, 'says that you know where all the agents are and that you have hidden them away and made Miss Sissins feel like she was to blame! Now I know that's nonsense and that you wouldn't do that to anyone, never mind some of your closest friends but can you please tell the truth to stop him talking.'

King shuffled his feet and raised an eyebrow, 'I have them locked up, hidden in plain sight and I won't be letting them out,' he replied with a sense of flippancy.

Clara's face melted, Natan smirked, Miss Sissins marched towards King and put her face right into his, 'Say that again!' Miss Sissins said, looking cross.

'You heard me,' King replied, 'I will not let them out, they will ruin my life's work. I will not let some fame-crazed fools turn everything I have built into a circus. You and I both heard them ten years ago, Sissins, they were going to sell themselves and this company out. *My* company, *my* agency, they were going to change everything.'

'But, Cole, my…' Miss Sissins couldn't speak, she felt sick.

Sophie and Yasmine stood at the back of everyone watching the drama play out. They had seen a different side of King in the few days they had been agents. He had given them so much this week, but it was all built on a lie. He had locked innocent people away for wanting nothing more than to get some credit. Sophie had spent enough time on the fence the last few days, working out what was right and what was wrong and there was no doubt in her mind that this was wrong.

In front of Sophie and Yasmine, Natan walked forward, stroking his chin, 'I told you so!'

Now seeing him completely out of the character of Mr Houghton, Sophie was finding it hard to see the good-natured head teacher who had worked with her throughout primary school.

Natan shot a finger at King who was just stood there not fazed by what was happening, 'This man is power mad and is only thinking of himself. Sissins, think of Cole, he has been locked up for ten years. You didn't lose him, you didn't cause the disappearance of the agents and ruin of all those people, he did and it's much worse for them than what you thought you'd done! They know where they are and how to get out but can't!'

Clara remained speechless, as did Sophie and Yasmine. They could see Miss Sissins was becoming more and more emotional. Her face was turning angry and her fists were clenched. She had tears streaming down her face, 'Tell me it's not true!' she demanded.

'It's true,' King said with no emotion on his face, 'Cole was not lost by you but hidden by me and you did not cause any harm or bring about any loss to anyone. I did.'

'What happened when I flicked that switch?' Jane asked, close to screaming.

'The first time?' King asked, 'No idea. Something with madam over there I think,' he said, pointing at Clara, 'The second time? Nothing. It just prompted me to turn all the agents into dust from inside Stratus.'

Miss Sissins howled a gut-wrenching howl of inner pain and relief. She couldn't take anymore and walked away from King, past the girls and stood weeping about fifty metres away from them. Sophie wondered who exactly Cole was, she could have a guess but that didn't mean it would be an accurate one.

King turned his gaze from Miss Sissins to Natan, 'I will not let them out Dale, this company is mine and it will not change. I will hold them there for a million years before I change my mind.'

Sophie saw that Clara was getting distressed and so put a hand on her shoulder. Sophie felt betrayed enough and she had only been led on for a week, Clara had been lied to for a lot longer than that!

'This company is not *yours*' Natan was getting annoyed now, '*we* built this company. *We* did!'

King showed his first emotion – disgust, 'Oh please don't insult me, Dale,' he was being very condescending and talking to Natan like he was an insect on the bottom of his shoe, 'I built this company, you were an ideas man who was in the right place at the right time, nothing more! Without you, I'd have succeeded. Without me, you would be nothing! In fact, without me, you *are* nothing!'

Natan was getting about ready to explode. King knew how to make him angry and it was clearly working. The girls took deep breaths, what would the next revelation be?

'Why the big need for secrecy, Al?' Natan asked, 'Why can't the world see us as international saviours? Tell everyone; we risked everything to keep them safe and got NOTHING!'

King smiled at this, 'That's the problem though isn't it. You don't actually want the human race to be made aware of the agents and see them rewarded. You just want the glory for you. You twisted those other agents around your finger and made them think that it would be them in the spotlight. That was never your intention was it? You might be able to twist everybody else, but not me Dale,' King barely paused before his final words, 'How are your wife and son?'

Natan froze. 'Don't bring them into this. We agreed we'd never bring each other's family into this. My wife and son are perfectly fine. Leave them out of this.'

'HA!' King fake laughed, 'FINE? They never see you, you're never home. Your son even begged you for an implant so that you might give him some attention and that was the start of it for you wasn't it! Your son with an implant – you could manipulate him into whatever you wanted. That's what you do! Use your own son and his desires to please you in order to further what *you* want! Let's be honest, he's a bit arrogant and not very bright! Thinks he's wonderful; look at that god-awful speech he did at school on Tuesday; all in an effort to get his daddy to love him more than he loved the idea of fame! I worry about just how far that boy will go in order to impress Daddy, who never takes any notice of him!'

Natan snapped, he grabbed Clara by the arm and pulled her across in front of him. Out of his pocket he pulled something small and white and held it up to Clara's head.

'Take that back!' Natan demanded.

'No Dale, I won't, put Clara down, she's done nothing wrong. These children are the future, on that you and I agree.'

'Do you know what this is? Natan asked, 'It's a dilator with The Nightmare Program loaded in again. This time though Clara will never wake up if I attach it to her avatar rather than her human form and will be trapped in her nightmare for ever. All you need to do is take back what you said and release those agents!'

With Miss Sissins oblivious to what was going on, Sophie and Yasmine were on their own. Clara was shaking, not convinced that King would save her in light of the new revelations. He had sacrificed people he had known a lot longer than her in order to save his company, she may as well be nothing to him and she knew it.

'We have to do something,' said Yasmine, 'we can't lose Clara again.'

'Agreed,' replied Sophie, whispering so as not to distract either King or Natan, 'and I know the only person that can help us!'

Sophie whispered something into Yasmine's ear and the pair zoned back into the office. All of the others in the room were far too distracted to notice and so, the stand-off continued.

Arriving back in Mr Houghton's office almost immediately, Sophie and Yasmine stood up from the chairs and ran as fast as they could towards the school's main entrance. It was about half an hour before school started and children had begun to arrive so that they could go to breakfast club while their parents hurried off to work.

Sophie peered in to see which children were there. Normally about ten of them all crowded round some small tables, stuffing their faces with toast, jam, cereal, whatever it was that breakfast club had on offer. Today, about four Foundation children were trying to spread jam on their toast and failing quite spectacularly. Mrs Tabard was trying desperately to keep up with orders and was somehow managing to juggle it very well. There was a lot going on, but Sophie couldn't see who she needed and turned to Yasmine.

'He's not here yet,' she said, frustrated.

'No, he isn't in there, but here he is, coming up the drive,' Yasmine interrupted, pointing out of the main door.

Walking up the drive, with bag on his back and book in his hand, was Reuben Houghton. Being year 6 now, Sophie could reach the buzzer that let people in and out of school. She buzzed the door open and shouted for Reuben to hurry up but he didn't hear her. Eventually, Yasmine held the door and Sophie ran outside to almost carry him into school! Whilst outside, Sophie noticed an extremely expensive car at the bottom of the driveway. For a split second, she could have sworn she recognised the silhouette of the driver, but she couldn't worry about that now.

Sophie let go of Reuben, Yasmine let go of the door and the three of them sat in the reception area of school. Opposite them was a large hatch where Mrs Tabard often scared off anybody that wanted to look round the school, or sometimes she liked to torment the parents by demanding money for trips get paid or chasing up excuses as to why children weren't at school. For now, though, the reception was empty. Sophie reached behind her and pulled the curtain to the hall across so that Mrs Tabard couldn't see that three children had 'gone rogue' round school.

Sophie then hurriedly got her words out, 'Reuben, we haven't got much time, you have to come with us.'

Reuben was more than slightly confused, 'Where?' he shrugged, 'and why would I want to go with you, Glitch?'

'It's your dad,' Yasmine replied with an equal amount of urgency in her voice as Sophie.

'What about him?' Reuben didn't sound worried at all.

'He's well, err…' Yasmine didn't quite know how to put it.

'I'm sending you a special link, Reuben, click on it and you will be able to see for yourself,' Sophie said.

Sophie zoned out to forward the link to send to Reuben which would allow him to project himself into Shadow and join the rest of them in the showdown and hopefully talk his dad round.

As Sophie zoned back in, they escorted Reuben to Mr Houghton's office.

Again, Sophie and Yasmine sat down where they had been before and pointed to Reuben to sit on the last remaining seat. Reuben did so, but was still slightly confused as to what was going on; why were the year 6 teacher, his dad and a random girl with jet-black hair all asleep in the head teacher's office.

Sophie explained to Reuben, 'Access your implant and click on the link.'

Reuben clearly did so as Sophie saw him zone out right in front of her and he didn't immediately come back. Yasmine had gone before Reuben, so Sophie followed suit. The three of them ended up exactly where they had left off – The Shop Floor.

Chapter 25 – Father and Son

All three appeared back exactly where Sophie and Yasmine had disappeared from, behind Dale Natan, who still had Clara round the neck across his body with a time dilator held, up against her head. King still stood with his hands behind his back, looking as calm and collected as he had done before. Clara let out a sharp wail, she was in huge distress. To her, she had lived an inescapable nightmare for six months and now she was under threat of doing it again without the possibility of coming back.

Sophie tried to attract Natan's attention but King cut her off first, 'I sacrificed all of my men and women last time, what makes you think taking the girl will have any effect on me? I have plenty of spares,' he said, pointing over at Sophie and Yasmine.

Natan seemed to shuffle and look round but not behind, he was getting desperate. Sophie had noticed that King was never going to change his mind and now it was beginning to dawn on Natan as well.

'Why? Why can't you have faith in humanity and let them see what we do! Why must it be kept secret from them; you and your ego?' Natan was clutching at straws.

'Don't try and make everyone else think you want what is best for humanity! This was all about greed and it always was. You wanted to be hero-worshipped and you brainwashed all the others into thinking the same thing! Everything worked before you meddled and everything will work again!' King was still being ruthless in his comments. He caught sight of Reuben stood behind his dad.

'Oh yes, your son!' King started again. Reuben moved forward slightly to get a clear listen on what was being said. 'Does he actually know *who* his father is? I'm guessing not after that performance on Tuesday. The way he grovelled for an implant, the patronising way he spoke to all the other children. You must be so embarrassed by him, desperate for his dad's affection when all his dad wants is to use his own son to get the entire world focused and lauding him! That's why he ended up with an implant, isn't it! Not because he's talented or clever but because you wanted *your* son and *your school* in the headlines. Reuben being there was a move solely designed to bring attention to you. You just loved having the cameras on *you*! Look at how you reacted when poor Sophie fainted, you loved every second of it, the opportunity for more fame, never mind Reuben!'

Reuben moved even closer, he could almost reach out and touch the man who Alton King was making out was his father now. He wanted desperately to know what was going on.

Natan rubbed the tears from his face and seemed to think carefully about his next words, he closed his eyes for a second, and then opened them, looking very apologetic and resigned to the fact that King wasn't going to change his mind. He let go of Clara and walked forward.

'Of course, it was all for me. Reuben's happiness never even crossed my mind; you know as well as I do the whole thing at the school was stage-managed. Getting me beamed around the world by all those film crews, people everywhere knew who I was – the way it should be. Fame and fortune, that's all I want. I even sold my own son for it and he doesn't even know!'

'Dad?' Reuben whispered through an inevitable onslaught of tears as it occurred to him who the man in front of him was but Reuben had no idea how or why his dad now looked the way he did.

Natan turned around slowly; he knew exactly what he was going to be faced with.

'Reuben?' he said through heartbroken eyes.

Miss Sissins stepped back into the group and could see exactly what was happening. She zoned out briefly and came straight back. While she was gone, Dale Natan morphed back into Mr Houghton and Reuben's heart sank.

Before Natan could do anything, Reuben disappeared.

He must have zoned back into the office, Sophie thought to herself. She wanted to go and fetch him but she couldn't leave the shop floor. Natan burst into tears, his plan was over and he had now lost his son as well, and glared back at King who simply shrugged his shoulders.

At this, Mr Houghton snapped, he charged straight at King and went to rugby tackle him off his feet. He left the ground and flew at him; arms outstretched aiming right for King's midriff. Just as he was about to make contact though, his hands went straight through King and Natan went catapulting across the floor like King wasn't even there. When he had finished sliding, Natan turned himself around but stayed sat on the floor.

'You're in your avatar?' Natan said as he sat on the floor. Then he stopped and thought for a moment, 'Where are you really then?' he asked.

Sophie shouted to Natan before he could work out any more about King's location. 'Where are the agents hidden Dale? King said they were hidden somewhere in plain sight, remember? We can still rescue all those people!'

Natan looked her square in the eye and realisation spread across his face, 'art?' he remembered from Sam's message that Sissins had forwarded to him.

'Yes,' replied Sophie, 'hidden in plain sight.'

'The painting in…' Natan disappeared.

Sophie turned to Yasmine, Clara and Miss Sissins.

'Where did he go?' Sophie screamed at computer-generated King.

King just smiled.

'Where he needs to be,' King replied and he promptly disappeared as well.

A red dot appeared in the corner of Sophie's eye. She clicked on it. The message read;

The Four of You,

It was never my intention for it to come to this. I have put up a temporary force field around the Shop Floor to prevent you from returning to school for a few minutes. After that time, you will see that Mr Natan and I are gone. Look after my agency; it is in the best hands with you four. I will deactivate my implant so please do not try to contact me, I won't get the message. Good luck, you children are the future.

Yours,

Alton King

In Mr Houghton's office back at school, a thin, grey haired man had attached a white ball to the side of Mr Houghton's head. Mr Houghton remained in a zoned-out state while the frail old man effortlessly picked him up and carried him out of the room. Walking down an empty corridor, because all the children were still just arriving at school on the playground, King walked through reception, out of the front door and towards his car, which he had parked right next to the main school door. He opened the back door and lay Mr Houghton down on the back seat. Sitting down in the driver's seat, King put on a pair of sunglasses and flicked behind his ear. In the blink of an eye, the old man who was there before was gone and had been replaced by someone completely new. Across the car park, he caught sight of Reuben Houghton, who had watched everything and was now trying to uselessly hide out of sight behind a bin. The new driver waved and the car drove off. Reuben ran off down the driveway in a panic.

Back on the Shop Floor, Sophie was thinking hard. Yasmine was consoling Clara, who was still upset so Miss Sissins went over and put her hand on Sophie's shoulder.

'All right, Soph?' she asked.

'Think so, just something about art in plain sight,' she replied, deep in thought.

'It could be any of them, don't think about it. We will get them all checked. We will find them,' Miss Sissins replied.

Sophie was thinking about when she had arrived in the reception area with Clara. That painting of the tall building that looked like Stratus had really caught her eye that day and she remembered the figures in it. She remembered that it looked like they were moving, waving even.

Making a leap of faith, Sophie ran for the exit and darted down the long white corridor towards reception. A smile appeared on her face; she knew where the agents were and Miss Sissins could get them out. She was going to rescue them all and the world would be ready for the return of the mythicals whenever that may be. On top of that she would have people who could potentially train her to make her even better and they could help Miss Sissins relieve some of the guilt. There was no stopping her; she got to reception and the grin spread across her face. As she looked at the painting though, the grin vanished. The people who were there before had gone. It was like they were never there. Miss Sissins caught up with her. She stood next to

Sophie and looked at the painting like she was. She tilted her head sideways and studied it more carefully.

'Has it always looked like that?' she asked.

'No,' replied Sophie, who was now fighting extreme disappointment, 'it hasn't.'

'That's one of the digital photos that Mr King invented. It's an interpretation of the Stratus building where all the data is stored for the implants. Without that the whole system would crash,' Miss Sissins explained. It's where King said I would be uploading the agents to…'

Sophie smiled a reluctant smile, 'So they were uploaded to Stratus then,' she said to herself. Then she turned around and walked away, patting Miss Sissins on the shoulder in a vague effort to console her of something she didn't even know she should be disappointed about.

Chapter 26 – Back to Reality

For the next five minutes, Sophie, Clara and Yasmine were stuck in the Shadow building. They remained on the Shop Floor not knowing quite what to do or what to say. Clara and Yasmine were sat on the floor; legs crossed playing with their fingers. Sophie was pacing the room, thinking about what King had written in that message. Had he really intended for the three girls to take over the defence of the world with the help of their teacher? That was basically what he had said. What had King done with the other agents and Mr Houghton? There was so much to process and she tried to talk about it with Clara and Yasmine but Clara still wasn't quite with it after her ordeal earlier. It seemed to have unearthed fresh scarring from the last few months and Yasmine was more focused on helping her. As a result, Sophie was left to think on her own.

At the start of the week she just wanted to be one of the older children, get access to the internet to better herself and help her to develop and make a better life for her and her family. Now she had her cousin back and here she was with a more than perfect opportunity to do just that. All that knowledge of aliens, wizards, mythical creatures and many more from her dad was at her disposal, complimented with the resources at Shadow. Sophie could see what a massive opportunity this was turning out to be but also couldn't help but think she was missing something. It was all a bit too good to be true.

As Sophie came to realise that almost the whole planet was now at her fingertips (exactly as she wanted), Miss Sissins walked back into the room with her hands in her pockets and a straight face. She meandered over to the girls and Clara and Yasmine stood up.

'You can go back to school now. The force field has been lifted and you need to get back,' Miss Sissins looked up from the floor and gave the girls a defeated smile.

'Who's Cole, Miss Sissins?' Yasmine asked.

Miss Sissins shuffled uncomfortably and looked like she was getting emotional again. She fell over her words at first but took a sharp intake of breath.

'My husband,' she looked like she wanted to go on but couldn't.

Clara suddenly softened to her again like she had done yesterday. All that criticising her, arguing that she should have opened her messages made Clara feel awful about what she had done to her and that it must have been so horrible for her not being able to talk to her husband because of King and Natan; all the while blaming herself.

Before anyone else could ask anything, Miss Sissins explained to them that they really needed to get back to school as the day was about to start and that if Mrs Tabard found them all zoned out in Mr Houghton's office there would be trouble.

'Tell Mrs Tabard that Mr Houghton has asked me to work in his office all day and that someone will need to cover my class,' Miss Sissins had gone back into teacher mode and the girls respected her more for it.

They all just nodded before Yasmine asked, 'What are you going to do, Miss?'

Miss Sissins shrugged her shoulders slightly; she looked like a woman who was out of her depth.

'It looks like I'm in charge of all this now. The safety of the world is in my hands. It's all up to me and at any minute the mythicals could return or aliens could invade. We should probably try and prevent that from happening!'

Sophie frowned but not aggressively, she knew her teacher better than that, 'Doesn't that excite you even a little bit?'

Miss Sissins clapped her hands together, 'Yeah, it does actually!'

'What are you going to do about... Mr... Sissins?' Clara asked not knowing if that was his proper name or not.

Miss Sissins smiled again, 'That's a story for another time. His conscience is alive and looking for me, I didn't think that twenty minutes ago. Now, get back to school.'

The girls smiled and hugged Miss Sissins before they all left and arrived back in Mr Houghton's office, opened the door and walked down the corridor to find Mrs Tabard in the reception. They were exhausted but didn't have time to think about that. When they reached the reception window, Yasmine tapped on it and Mrs Tabard, who was having a few minutes off from washing up after breakfast club, turned and looked at them.

'What are you three doing in here?' she screeched, 'You should be on the playground waiting for the whistle.'

Not deterred by Mrs Tabard's abruptness, Yasmine relayed the lie that Miss Sissins had told her to.

'She wants cover! The children are coming in in five minutes!' Mrs Tabard clearly had no idea that there were much more important things going on in the world at the moment but Yasmine couldn't very well say that!

Mrs Tabard sifted through some papers on the office desk in an effort to find a phone number to ring someone to come in. Part way through, she stopped and a gleeful look spread across her face, 'I'll cover her.'

'Pardon?' Yasmine asked, completely taken aback by Mrs Tabard's suggestion, 'You?'

'Yes Yasmine, why not?' Mrs Tabard asked looking most put out at the fact that Yasmine couldn't imagine her teaching.

Yasmine shrugged as she could think of worse ideas, all the children knew of Mrs Tabard's dream.

Mrs Tabard looked through the window at who else was with Yasmine and Sophie, 'Betts!'

'Yes, Mrs Tabard,' Clara replied, smiling.

'I thought you'd left...' Mrs Tabard said as Clara smiled again in response, '... You're going to mess up the register!'

Clara smiled again and the girls fell about laughing.

Mrs Tabard looked through the window again and counted, 'Isn't there normally four of you? Where's Katie?'

The girls all looked at each other. Katie had tried to talk to them before they arrived at school that morning but the girls had shrugged her off. It was time to go and find the fourth member of their quartet, bring her up to speed and make her an agent. They had neglected her all week and not spoken to her. She hadn't been given an implant when Sophie and Yasmine had, she had been left at school by herself during the blackout, wanted to talk to them all urgently and been ignored since - it was time to be a friend again. The girls walked towards the door that would lead them out onto the playground.

Mrs Tabard shouted after them, 'Oh wait, hold on, there was a message sent directly to Mr Houghton's office yesterday evening saying that Katie wouldn't be here today.'

The girls stopped and looked at each other. They had seen her earlier that morning in her school uniform so why wouldn't she be here?

'Oh, ok Mrs Tabard; see you in a few minutes,' Yasmine said calmly in order to hide the girls' concern.

Sophie opened the door to the playground and the three wandered out. Immediately, they scanned the playground for Katie, hoping that there had been a mistake. None of them could see her.

They walked down the stairs onto the playground, fighting their way through the parents of Foundation children who still, even after a week, couldn't stop crying that their little babies were now off to school. They surveyed the playground and had to admit that Katie wasn't there.

Before they could concoct a plan or begin to hypothesise about where Katie was, all three of them were faced with flashing red lights in the corner of their eyes. They all found a quiet area of the playground and zoned out one at a time. All three of them were met with the same message:

Girls,

There is a serious problem here at Shadow. Get here, now!

Miss S

'What do we do?' Yasmine asked.

Sophie had already processed everything, 'We can't zone out, Mrs Tabard knows we're here and so we can't get out of lessons. School starts in about two minutes and we haven't got any time dilators, meaning we can't help Miss Sissins and we also have no way of finding out where Katie is!' Sophie came up for air before the horrible realisation kicked in, 'There's only one thing for it...'

'What?' Clara asked.

Sophie replied with grave fear in her voice, 'We have to go to school!'

Chapter 27 – One More Problem to Solve

As the morning dragged on, Sophie, Yasmine and Clara made plans to try and zone out at break time. They would all find a secluded part of the school field and lie down on the grass, pretending to be looking at the sky; it would be unlikely anyone would disturb them. However, ten minutes before break time, the rain started falling like the weather itself wanted to stop them.

Mrs Tabard, who was enjoying the opportunity to cover the class so much and was teaching column addition in a way so over the top that she could have been nominated for an acting award, almost sensed the rain coming and did that thing that lunchtime workers always do. As the first drop hit the window, 'Wet break!' she shouted in a tone that implied she enjoyed breaking the news to the class.

Tuts and groans were let out by every child in the room, whereas Mrs Tabard seemed to revel in the idea of having the class for even longer, allowing her to educate the children even more than she had done. This meant that Sophie, Yasmine and Clara had to think again; dinner time looked out of the question as the rain was still falling and there was no way they would be able to find a quiet place.

Next lesson passed but the rain didn't. Then, so did dinner time but still the rain fell. At random points throughout the afternoon, more and more red dots appeared in their eyes. When Mrs Tabard wasn't looking, the girls would quickly zone out, read what they said and then come back into the classroom. Every single one of the messages was from Miss Sissins, who desperately needed them back at Shadow. While Mrs Tabard spent about five minutes talking to one of the boys at the front of the room, Clara really quickly typed –

Why can't you come and get us? You're only in Mr Houghton's office?

Miss Sissins didn't reply.

With five minutes left in the day, Mrs Tabard finally told everyone to start packing away. The girls knew that they were about to be given the freedom that they needed. For a whole day, the three of them would have given nothing more than to be able to zone out to go and see what the huge situation was that was developing at Shadow. Now they could almost taste their freedom.

The three had agreed that going back to Mr Houghton's office would be crying out for trouble and so agreed that, because Yasmine's house was the largest and the closest, they would go to hers and hide out in her bedroom. As soon as everyone had tidied up and Mrs Tabard had dismissed them, the girls grabbed their bags and made a run for the exit. Being able to walk home on their own meant they didn't have to contend with Clara's dads or Sophie's parents asking unwanted questions. They ran all the way to Yasmine's house. Her mum, Zoe, was in the kitchen and dad was on a call in the other room when they all burst in.

'Mum, can you let Sophie and Clara's parents know that they're here, please!' Yasmine asked as the three ran upstairs.

'Clara? Hasn't she left?' Zoe asked, surprised.

'No, she's here with us,' Yasmine shouted as the three rounded the top of the stairs and ran for Yasmine's room.

'Do you want a drink, the three of you?' Zoe shouted, now at the bottom of the stairs.

'No thanks,' Yasmine bellowed back and shut her bedroom door.

'They'll be teenagers soon,' Zoe said to herself as she walked back to the kitchen, smiling and shaking her head.

The three of them got comfy and zoned out. What they saw when they awoke gave them an idea as to why Miss Sissins had been panicking. They arrived in the reception area with the painting, but whereas before everything had been white and clean and new, now there were flashing red lights, sirens wailing and large signs on the walls flashing 'WARNING!' in huge red letters.

Clara ran down the white corridor, as they had done when they first brought Clara back to be checked out, Sophie and Yasmine followed, not at all sure where they were running to.

About 300 metres down the corridor, Clara stopped and put her hand over the wall on the right. The wall parted and revealed yet another "hidden" room. Clara ran straight in and, once again, Sophie and Yasmine walked in with a slight fear of the unknown. Still the lights flashed and the sirens wailed.

As Sophie walked in, she saw that this room wasn't shiny and new like the others she had seen. This was older; it had a staircase through the middle with bannisters on either side. At the top of the stairs was a large balcony, which had screen after screen of data and information flashing on it. Clara had run all the way to the top where Miss Sissins was stood, looking extremely rigid. Sophie and Yasmine walked up behind her, taking in as much as they could. About half way up the stairs was another level, which contained smaller screens that seemed to have cameras that were following certain people around in cities. Sophie watched as closely as she could but couldn't make any of them out but it did seem like the people had no idea they were on the screen.

Finally, arriving at the top, Sophie and Yasmine joined in the conversation with the other two.

'If I let go of this then they all get out,' Miss Sissins was looking extremely flustered.

'What's happening?' Sophie asked.

Clara turned to the pair of them, 'Someone has broken into Zatvor.'

'What exactly is Zatvor?' Sophie asked; this was about the third time she'd heard it mentioned but still wasn't much the wiser as to what it was. She did recall her dad saying something about a prison called Sadcore though.

'Well, you know how we protect Earth from the worst of the worst,' Miss Sissins began, still clinging on to the buttons and levers for dear life, 'we need somewhere to house the creatures that we catch. That is what Zatvor is for.'

'A prison then?' Sophie asked, knowing full well she was already right having remembered what Clara had said to her earlier.

'Yes, and someone has broken in to it,' Miss Sissins turned to say, not moving her finger.

'Why does someone want to break *in* to your prison?' Sophie asked, trying to gain as much information as she could.

'Probably to break someone out?' thought Yasmine, shrugging her shoulders.

'Yes, Yazz,' Miss Sissins replied, 'Dale Natan must have got in there somehow and now plans to unleash every mythical we've ever caught meaning Mr King has no choice but to release the agents on Natan's terms!'

'But why has it taken him all day? Your first message came through this morning, is he still trying?' Sophie asked.

Miss Sissins tried to mop her brow on her shirt but couldn't quite reach, 'The first signs of a break-in came in this morning, alarms were triggered and doors were opened. I put the whole thing into emergency shutdown, which stopped him for a few minutes but, as he used to work here and knows his way around, it didn't take long for Mr Natan to hack it again. More doors opened and we got closer to a full breakout.'

'So, what's stopping them now?' Yasmine asked.

'They still have one door to open – the main front door. If that were to open then it would let out every creature we have ever caught. The world would be under threat from countless beings and demons. Mr Natan has been fighting me from inside the control room in the prison, trying to open it, however as long as this button is pressed, that door stays shut. He hasn't tried for a while, I think he's waiting for me to tire but as soon as I let go, he will be hacking away again. We have to stop him before he can let everyone out. With no agents and the worst of the evil creatures roaming the Earth, it would spell disaster.'

'Isn't the forcefield around Earth due to fail soon meaning the world will be under threat anyway?' Sophie asked.

'Yes,' replied Miss Sissins, 'but the way that Natan is sabotaging the system like this would deactivate that force field early. The world would be opened up not just to creatures from Zatvor but every mythical creature the world or even the universe has ever seen! All that would be in their way would be you three!'

Clara, Sophie and Yasmine looked at each other. 'Are you ready for your first proper mission?' Clara asked with a twinkle in her eye, 'Ready to stop Natan once and for all?'

Sophie and Yasmine also couldn't help but smile. They were going to go and save the world.

Miss Sissins said authoritatively, 'Clara, give them a link.'

Clara zoned out to type the link, and then reappeared as it came through.

Miss Sissins was clearly revelling in her new role as leader, 'There should be some time dilators kept in the room he's in. You need to get one and stick it to the side of his head,' she then said.

'Will time move slower or faster for him?' Sophie asked.

'Much slower, one minute for us will be about one nanosecond for him,' Miss Sissins replied.

Sophie nodded and understood what needed to be done. Clara smiled at the opportunity of revenge and Yasmine simply said, 'Let's go get him.'

The three of them all zoned out of Shadow and, still wearing their school uniforms as avatars, arrived in Zatvor.

Chapter 28 – Breaking In

Sophie, Yasmine and Clara looked upon their new surroundings. They were on what they guessed must have been about the second level of a multi-storey building. If they looked up, they could see more and more floors, with grease and grime hanging off the handrails, like looking up the inside of the world's dirtiest skyscraper. When they looked downwards they were faced with a cesspit of wrongdoing. Just from a quick scan round, they could see a variety of different creatures all looking hard and unjust. Sophie's gaze was immediately taken by three huge ogres that dominated the centre of the floor. They were gargantuan and had a mixture of purple, green and grey in their wart-ridden skin. Around their waists they wore rags and over their shoulders they carried enormous clubs that they were using to attack anything smaller that came within their reach. Their faces were dominated by hideous noses, evil eyes and repugnant teeth that were yellow and decrepit. Sophie couldn't begin to imagine them in the real world and didn't dare think about the damage they could do.

Strangely, the next thing that Sophie noticed was something that could have passed for a human just a few meters to the girls' right. Curled up in a ball in the corner of the room was a man with bright white hair down to his waist – it clearly hadn't been cut for many years.

He was sat down and his hands and arms were wrapped around his knees in front of him. This wasn't a scary man but a scared man. Sophie walked up to him and went to bend down next to him. Unsure of what creature he was, Sophie racked her brain for anything that her dad had told her about creatures with bright white hair but came up with nothing. As she leant closer to see if he was ok, the man suddenly turned and stared at Sophie, dead in the eye. His eyes were a piercing red and Sophie stepped back in astonishment.

The man had tears in his eyes and simply uttered the sentence, 'Condenar is coming!'

Once Sophie lost the man's gaze, he said it again and again and again.

Sophie put her hand out and touched the man on the shoulder, this man wasn't a danger, 'It's ok, I'm Sophie. I'm here to help.'

Feeling a sudden change in emotion from frightened to sad, Sophie could sense that the man didn't belong in this prison so went to reassure him some more but all the man started doing was saying, 'Condenar is coming but Sophie will help!' over and over again.

Clara had heard so much about this place but she had only ever seen it in photos that Miss Sissins and King had shown her. She recognised some of the faces that she had read about in her research that she had done over the last few months. Nothing could have prepared her though for what it actually looked like inside. Everyone seemed to have free rein over where they could go – the complete opposite of what she had imagined a prison to be. Clara had always imagined a prison holding its inmates in cells but with the departure of all agents – including prison guards ten years ago, clearly the mythicals had got out and were living "freely" within the confines of the prison.

However, this wasn't a normal prison. From the reading she had done, she knew that the huge door was there to keep everyone in and that the dampeners had been placed randomly around the inside to prevent any powers from helping people to escape or to cause too much trouble. It meant that mind readers couldn't mind read, teleporters couldn't teleport and speedsters couldn't run fast. It was a minute version of the field Miss Sissins had used to shield the planet but it had been enough to keep the inmates inline for the best part of a decade.

Sophie and Yasmine both looked at Clara for help, 'What do we do?' Sophie asked, almost completely at a loss. The man she had tried to talk to had wrapped himself up again and was now muttering, 'Condenar is coming but Sophie will help!'

'So where do we go?' asked Sophie, drawing her attention away from the mythical.

'I can help with that!' Miss Sissins said, 'A little way to the left of the main door that is below you is the control room. Natan must be in there, playing about with the settings, trying to hack open the door to let everyone out.'

Sophie looked to the left of the huge door. Sure enough, there was much smaller door, which was almost camouflaged in against the wall.

'Why hasn't anyone else gone in there before to try and unlock the door?' Sophie asked.

'It was on a perception filter,' Miss Sissins replied.

A few days ago, Sophie would have had no idea what she was talking about but now she knew instantly.

'But we can see it?' she said, knowing what the reason for this was.

'Mr Natan must have broken it when he broke in, which means, just like Clara's house, everyone can now see it. We need to be quick; it won't take the inmates long to notice something is afoot with three ten-year-old human girls walking around. Then all it takes is one of the ogres there to start banging on the exit door – that large one next to the control room – and before we know it, they're all outside and the world is in terrible danger!'

The three girls agreed and set about getting down off the second floor down to the ground. The staircase was round a 90 degree turn. Then all they needed to do was walk across the mythical-filled floor to the door and disappear into the control room. The three of them took a deep breath and turned to their left.

Trying desperately *not* to look like three school girls in a prison full of ghastly creatures, the girls walked as casually as their nerves allowed them to. All around them there were screams of pain and suffering and more horrendous creatures came into their eye line. There were sirens and ghosts, gremlins and trolls of all shapes and sizes. Trying to look normal, the girls reached the stairs and began to climb down slowly.

About half way down, Clara stopped as a creature flew into her view and started cackling to her.

'Who are you?' the creature asked. It had a gremlin type head with crystal blue eyes, long scaly fingers and enormous bat-like wings. It also had a tail like a snake and horns that were at least twice the height of its head. 'I know this prison better than anyone and I ain't ever seen you round here.'

'That's a slither,' Miss Sissins said in their ears, 'really nosey creature, thinks it knows everything; was used to do the dirty work of giants. Just tell him your new inmates and to mind his own business.'

Yasmine took it upon herself to march to the front of the line; 'We're new here!' she started by saying in a very aggressive tone, 'best watch your back, we're dangerous!'

Sophie and Clara looked at each other, wondering what on Earth their friend was doing; they had no choice but to follow her lead and had to put on tough voices as well to agree with her.

'Why's you dressed like that? You come out of school or something?' The creature continued to probe.

'You what?' Yasmine screeched in a tone that she wouldn't think about speaking in normally as her parents would have really told her off, 'You say that again and you'll be sorry! This is the battle armour of the Valkyrie; the greatest band of female warriors to ever live. Look us up!'

The slither thought for a moment as he seemed to be racking his brain. Sophie and Clara were starting to get nervous, this was taking too long.

'I've heard of you! Don't remember you wearing purple though!' he replied.

'Upgrade!' Yasmine said, right in the creature's face, almost like she was enjoying it.

At that, the slither flew off. He grunted slightly and huffed like he had been most put out. Yasmine slipped slightly but held onto the rail as the enormity of what she had just done began to sink in.

'Where did that come from?' Clara asked.

'I remembered your dad mentioning them once, Soph. Good job I did really!' Yasmine replied, struggling for breath.

'That's not entirely what I meant!' Clara said, holding her friend up, stopping her from collapsing in shock.

With no time for Yasmine to recover, the girls continued down the stairs and made their way across the main floor. They made sure to stay out of the way of the ogres as they were just the right size for them to snack on. They did though catch sight of even more woeful creatures. Werewolves were roaming the floor and centaurs with battle scars all over their bodies patrolled around the edge. Inches from the door, the girls heard another, more human like voice talk to them.

'You girls! You know somethings wrong don't you!' The girls turned to see what, at first, they presumed was a woman in a white flowing dress with red hair. On closer inspection though, it was obvious that although it had the body of a man, its face was pink and looked like a dolphin with what appeared to be black mascara rubbed all round his eyes, 'I have been in here for what feels like countless decades and my magic has never worked, now though I am just starting to get an insight into the minds of some people here!'

'You're up Yasmine!' said Miss Sissins in their ears, 'he's one of the magic folks that reside here; originally found in the Amazon rainforest - an encantado, he could potentially read your mind if his powers are returning, be careful!'

Yasmine strolled up, all confident once again, 'Sorry, we don't know what you're talking about,' she said assertively.

'No, you do, I think you're looking for something,' the encantado said calmly; he looked her up and down and studied her eyes closely.

Yasmine shifted uncomfortably, she had been caught off guard and the creature could see that.

'You don't belong here, you're here to find something or someone and then you're leaving! These powers are getting stronger, almost like someone's slowly turning the dampeners off!'

Yasmine was lost and out of her depth and Clara could see this. So, she grabbed Yasmine's arm and pulled her out of the way.

'Look, we're inmates here, just like you. So, leave us alone!' Clara whispered threateningly so as not to attract attention.

'No, you aren't' the encantado started again. Suddenly, his eyes flickered and his head fell backwards before shooting back forward again and his eyes changed from black to green.

'How's your *real* dad, Clara?' the creature said in an abrupt, gravelly tone.

Clara just stared at him, completely dumbfounded. Her parents were one topic that she never spoke about and the one topic her friends knew never to discuss. Sophie knew that Clara had been adopted by her uncles when she was a baby but that was it.

'Answer me!' the encantado demanded and the girls remained silent in shock.

Near the door, a sorcerer was conjuring up a spell that he hadn't been able to do for years.

The encantado continued its rant, 'I am the sole survivor of the banishment of the child-snatchers and former occupant of the underworld. You will answer my question! For years I have been trapped here by a man with dark hair like yours in here for the mere crime of...'

The creature's eyes suddenly turned back to normal and went back to studying the girls before it floated off, completely unaware of the scene it had caused.

'Let's get in shall we,' said Sophie, trying to calm a now even more tense situation, however, as she reached for the handle and turned it. A voice let out a shriek from far away.

'LOOK AT THOSE GIRLS!'

The three of them turned around. The slither was at the top of the stairs pointing and shouting at them. Every other inmate turned to look at what it was pointing at. What they all saw was three girls stood next to a door that none of them had ever seen before. Beyond the door they could see flashing lights but not a lot else. Silence descended.

'Get. In,' said Clara without moving her lips.

Sophie moved to go inside but before she could even move, the whole prison was bounding up to the door. As quick as a flash, Sophie, Yasmine and Clara flew through the door and pulled it shut behind them.

'Locked it, but it won't hold,' said Miss Sissins's voice in their ears, 'Get Natan and I'll somehow help you get out! Right now, it's stop him or the mythicals come back with nobody to stop them but you three!'

The girls looked round the room. It was still horrible and messy and clearly hadn't been touched for years, but it looked a lot more futuristic and modern than the other part of the prison they had seen. There were monitors on the walls and buttons waiting to be pressed. Sophie clocked the drawers that Miss Sissins had said contained spare time dilators. The monitors seemed to show different sections of the prison but that wasn't what the girls found themselves staring at. In the one chair in the room sat a figure with their head in their hands. A sniffling sound was coming from them and Sophie could see that their feet didn't even reach the floor as they were perched on a chair designed for someone much bigger. Sophie, Yasmine and Clara walked up to them as the person wiped their eyes on their purple sleeve. The three gasped as Katie's distraught face looked solemnly upon them.

Chapter 29 – What!

Yasmine nearly fell over with the shock of what was in front of her. Clara put her hands over her mouth to keep in the scream she wanted to make. Sophie just stared at her friend. Katie looked round at all three of them and the worry and fright leapt out of her eyes. The first to step forward, Sophie, went to put a hand of reassurance on her friend's shoulder but then pulled back. Katie's uniform was muddied and her hair was in a state. She was also sat with one foot under the other, almost like one of her legs wasn't there – it looked frighteningly uncomfortable to Sophie but that was the least of her worries!

After carefully thinking about it, Sophie plucked up the courage to talk first, her brain had so many questions to ask; she hadn't known where to start.

'Katie, what are you doing here?' Sophie asked with as much understanding and reassurance as she could muster.

Katie looked Sophie square in the eye and again cleared her face of tears, 'I don't know.'

'OK, *why* are you here?' Sophie asked.

Shuffling in her chair, Katie looked at the ceiling and took a deep breath, 'Mr Houghton told me this was what I had to do.'

Sophie, Yasmine and Clara looked at each other and tried to process what they were hearing. The screams outside had faded due to sound-proof walls, as such, the room was eerily silent.

'What do you mean?' Clara asked, 'What did Mr Houghton tell you?' Clara wasn't sure exactly what Katie knew about anything the girls had lived over the course of the week or how much she knew about why she was where she was right now.

'Mr Houghton said that he had spoken to my dad over his implant. I haven't heard from him for years but Mr Houghton said that he had contacted him at school and wanted to possibly, maybe, want to see me again,' Katie sniffled,

Sophie, Yasmine and Clara began to shift uncomfortably where they stood. Yasmine could stand no more and rested her arm on the side of Katie's chair. Clara pushed her hair off her face and held her hands on the top of her head. Sophie probed for more.

'Then what...'

'The week went on, I spent the afternoon at school with Mr Houghton and a few other children the afternoon of the blackout. When you both went home, he told me he had spoken to my dad again and that he was really interested in coming to see me but that you becoming so famous Sophie had put him off. Mr Houghton said that my dad didn't want the friend of a famous child, he wanted a daughter he could be proud of, someone who had done something world-changing,' Katie looked at Sophie, not with anger or jealousy but with calm eyes. Getting this off her chest was clearly helping. 'Mr Houghton said that if I was to do something for him, it would make me stand out and that my dad would love me even more and that he would want to see me again.'

'What did Mr Houghton say?' Yasmine asked.

'That by coming here and pressing these buttons in the correct order at the correct time I would free some people who had been wrongly put in prison and that the world would welcome their return, some agents or something. He said it was my duty and that I would be as famous as you Sophie like my dad wants me to be. I did try and tell you this morning but you ignored me again. I wanted you to come with me and help but you didn't want to know.'

Sophie stepped back in horror. Mr Houghton had lied to Katie in an effort to get her to release the prisoners and the three of them had ignored her. Sophie thought about it logically, if you release the prisoners, someone has to put them back, to capture them and put them back would require agents trained in missions like that. That was it, if all the prisoners were set free then King would have no choice but to release the agents because there was no way the three girls would be able to deal with it all by themselves. This would mean that Dale Natan would get what he had always wanted – he could go public and earn admiration for everything they did. What kind of monster would manipulate a shy, 10-year-old girl who just missed her dad though? What was it Miss Sissins had said earlier? - One of the most dangerous men in the known worlds. Sophie could now see clearly what she had meant about the lies and the manipulation.

'How did you get here?' Clara asked.

'The other day, when you all left Mr Houghton's office during lunch time when we had to stay in, I was left behind while you went back to the classroom. Mr Houghton gave me information on getting here, how to get in and what to do once I was here. It was all pretty easy. I tried to tell you but you kicked me out the classroom. Then I tried to say something this morning but you weren't bothered.'

Katie was relaxing even more. The familiarity of her friends had calmed her immensely. It alarmed Sophie that to Katie this was relatively normal.

'But, where are we?' asked Yasmine, 'I mean I know we're in Zatvor – the most dangerous prison on the planet, but where exactly is it?'

'I don't know,' Katie replied, 'I can't really remember getting here; it's all a bit hazy, I think I was brought here. How did *you* get here?'

'We aren't here, we're in Yasmine's room,' Sophie explained, 'these are just projections of us, through our implants.'

Katie looked a bit disappointed, since her friends had arrived she thought, via some miracle, that she wasn't in this on her own; to find out that her friends were here but weren't upset her.

'So, I am on my own and you can leave whenever you want?' Katie asked, disappointed.

Horrified at what her friend was being forced to think, Sophie stepped forward again, determined to help her friend out after ignoring her so much, 'You are *not* on your own Katie, stop what you're doing and we can figure out a way to get us all out.'

Katie looked confused by this, she had no intention of stopping, her dad wanted her to do this, he had told Mr Houghton, and she wasn't going to pass up the opportunity to see him again now. 'But, what about my dad?' she asked innocently, 'I want to see him again.'

Sophie, Yasmine and Clara looked at Katie; she had believed every word of what Mr Houghton had told her. A new problem now presented itself – how to convince her she had been lied to – that her dad still wanted nothing to do with her but to do it a way that didn't upset her so much that she pressed the button anyway!

Sophie gestured for Yasmine and Clara to step away from Katie for a minute so that they could have a silent chat. Katie went back to pressing her buttons which would unlock the prison and send the world into the type of chaos that it hadn't seen in a decade. In their ears, Miss Sissins's voice appeared.

'Girls, have you got Natan?' she asked.

'Not exactly' Sophie replied.

As quick as they could, the girls explained the situation to Miss Sissins; understandably, she wasn't entirely sure that what she was hearing was accurate, but she had no choice but to believe it. Katie was still sat at the screen typing away, following instructions that Mr

Houghton had written and given to her, still convinced that it was what her dad wanted.

'What are our options?' Clara asked.

There were a few seconds of silence over the radio while Miss Sissins thought, 'You've got lots but all of them are bad!'

Sophie, Clara and Yasmine had already worked out that much.

'Give us all of them,' Clara said.

It was becoming clear that she had done stuff like this before, in the weeks prior to Sophie and Yasmine coming along. She sounded professional, comfortable with what she was saying and doing; she wasn't fazed at all! Sophie was absorbing it all but Yasmine was decidedly more agitated at the mess she had found their friend, who the three of them hadn't treated as one over the last few days, in.

'1. You stop Katie typing, I lock the door, you three can get out but Katie is stuck there and will be devoured by the prisoners once they finally batter the door down.'

'No,' replied Clara and Sophie, not even thinking about it.

'OK, 2. Katie stops unlocking the door, the three of you stay with her and try to fight off an oncoming storm of mythicals when they break that door down. When you don't win, which you won't, the prisoners will have access to the control panel and there are plenty of characters in there who are capable of unlocking the door and letting themselves out. You three of course can get out eventually but Katie will be eaten alive or killed in some other horrific way. '

Clara gave this some half-hearted thought, but again, almost immediately, replied, 'Is there no way at all to get Katie out?'

'No,' Miss Sissins decided to cut a long story short, 'Look, I could list other options but the situation in a nutshell is; those prisoners now know where the hidden control room is because they saw you open it. They *are* getting in there, like it or not. They *will* open the door, one way or another. I can't keep them all out. So, are you going to try and save Katie or are the three of you going to go and leave her behind?'

The three of them looked at each other, their personalities and even their appearances had changed so much since the start of all this. Clara was a hardened, experienced head on very young, 10-year-old, shoulders. Sophie had the knowledge and experiences she had craved and was learning so much more than she could have ever wished for and Yasmine had grown in confidence so much, that the flamboyant, over the top girl that appeared occasionally at school was so much more the real Yasmine now.

'There's no decision to make. We aren't leaving her behind,' Sophie said with steely determination, really rising to the occasion and the needs of her friend.

As Sophie finished, so did Katie. The banging on the door got slightly louder as the sound proofing started to fail. Dust was emanating from the door as it was about to fall off its hinges.

'There we go, just the final sequence left to type I think,' said Katie kicking back on her chair, 'oh my dad is going to be so proud of me. Perhaps he might even get back together with my mum!'

Sophie pursed her lips in anger and determination, thinking about how Mr Houghton had lied to and manipulated her friend, all in an effort to get what he wanted. She could stand no more and, having analysed the situation again, realised there was an option that would get Katie out unharmed but also do the unthinkable to Earth. Sophie didn't need to think about it but she did need to tell Yasmine and Clara. She knew exactly what she had to do to save her friend and she walked over to the back of Katie's chair, took a time dilator out of one of the drawers and stuck it on the side of Katie's head. Immediately, Katie stopped and appeared to doze off.

'What did you do that for?' Yasmine asked.

'It isn't fair to have Katie be responsible for what I'm about to do,' Sophie said.

Yasmine and Clara both looked baffled.

'I'm about to release all of the evils that used to cause damage all over the world. The stories, the nightmares that parents lived through are about to become real again so that we can save our friend. Dale Natan's plan has worked in that he will get the mythicals released but he won't get his agents back as only King knows where they are, it'll be up to us. Katie can't and won't live with that. All those times we have ignored her this week - I'm going to have to put it right. I'm about to be responsible for everything that comes next; the world will have to face the consequences of me saving our friend.'

It took Yasmine a few seconds to realise what Sophie was talking about, Clara got there just before Yasmine and understood what Sophie was about to do. It was inevitable, they were never going to leave their friend – not when her being here was partly their fault. They would never be able to live with themselves and, in that moment, they knew what they had to do.

'It'll be us against every evil imaginable,' Clara said, resigned to the understanding of what Sophie was now about to do.

'We can't do it alone,' Yasmine added, having also figured it out, 'We will need others. Just us and Miss Sissins won't be enough.'

Sophie nodded in agreement, 'Yes... we will recruit and rebuild, but King and Natan agreed on one thing and so do I. Children are the future. We will find others to help and we will defeat anything that comes our way. Won't we, Miss Sissins!'

'Of course, Soph,' said the voice in their ears, 'now, do it, because I can't hold that door into your room any longer.'

'What about the force field round the Earth?' Yasmine asked.

'The code that Katie has put into that computer is the code to deactivate everything...' Miss Sissins confirmed what she had suspected earlier.

The three girls looked at each other but nobody could speak a word. The mythicals were about to come back and the Earth was about to open up to any aliens or mythical creatures that wanted it.

At that, Sophie still couldn't see why that should stop her saving her friend and so turned to the control panel. She looked at Katie's piece of paper and keyed in the last few instructions. It was, as Katie said, really simple and easy to do. As soon as Sophie pressed the final key, the banging noise stopped and a loud whirring sound took its place. It sounded like an enormous garage door opening. Waiting a few minutes to make sure the room outside was completely empty, they held out for complete silence. Eventually, when the silence had arrived, between the three of them, they opened the door out into the prison again and Yasmine and Clara carried Katie out with her arms over their shoulders. Arriving in the large room that a few minutes earlier had been swarming with the worst the universe had to offer, it was now unnervingly quiet. Nothing remained. To the left of them they could see faint sunlight through the enormous door that had allowed the creatures to escape. They carried Katie towards the light and turned into it. In front of them, Sophie caught sight of the man with white hair and red eyes hobbling away from the prison.

'Condenar is coming but Sophie will help,' he kept repeating as he slowly shuffled off over the field in front of him and into a small group of tall trees. Before he disappeared, he caught Sophie's eye and nodded in acknowledgement of the help she had given. Neither Yasmine nor Clara noticed him as they were too busy helping carry Katie out. 'You can't save them all,' he finally said and he disappeared amongst the trees.

Once the group had gone out through the main door, they were greeted by rolling green fields, a solitary road leading across the front of them and the wood which the unknown man had walked off into. Sophie also couldn't help but notice the gorgeous shade of light blue that was completely unfamiliar to her. It was like a filter had been taken off the sky, and Sophie was seeing it in its true colour for the first time in her life.

Miss Sissins had already dispatched one of the cars that Sophie had seen on the Shop Floor on her first visit to Shadow. This would take Katie home to her mum. The three girls agreed to wait with Katie until the car arrived, put her in it, then take off the time dilator and let her sleep all the way home.

The girls looked behind them to look at the prison from the outside but there was nothing there, just vast, rolling hills with the sunset on the horizon, Miss Sissins told them that there was a fresh perception filter operating around it so that it could never be discovered. As the three sat on the grass and the sun finished its journey for the day, they discussed plans for the future and Miss Sissins sent them some documents that gave information on what creatures had escaped. They sounded horrendous. For a group of ten-year-olds, it was going to be a monumental task. No adult would believe what had happened even if they tried. They were in this on their own; King had gone, he'd take Natan with him along with the agents of Shadow, who were the only people specially trained at this. They had Miss Sissins but they were going to have to learn everything as they went along and fast! The incident with the Minotaur had helped but Sophie couldn't help but feel that longer, harder days were ahead. They had reshaped the world with what they had just done and no one would ever know it was them.

As the car arrived, they lay Katie down in the back of it and took off the time dilator. The three girls had been waiting for about two hours but to Katie it was only two minutes. She yawned whilst lying on the seat and dozed off almost immediately. The car pulled off and the girls agreed to zone back into Yasmine's bedroom again.

When they came around, standing there, waiting for them, were Amelia, Tom, Yasmine's dad, Nicholas, and Clara's dad, Matthew.

'Finished playing about with your new toys, have you?' Amelia asked.

'Mum, I was going to tell you...' Sophie began.

'Don't worry dear, it's what you always wanted and I couldn't be happier for you. Just don't waste all your time on it! There's a life out there to live you know!'

Sophie looked at her dad. He was stood with his left arm across his stomach and his right hand stroking his jaw, 'Good trip?' he asked, raising his eyebrows and talking in a tone that was normally saved for when Sophie had done something wrong. The smile was wiped off Sophie's face for a split second but it returned when Tom stepped forward and gave her an almighty hug and kissed her head.

'Time to say goodbye... for now,' Tom told Sophie.

Sophie turned and smiled at Yasmine and Clara who just smirked to each other, realising that they weren't in trouble with their parents.

Matthew took Clara's hand and gave her a hug. Fortunately, Miss Sissins had told Clara that she had implanted memories in her dads' minds about her getting an implant and that they were absolutely fine with it.

Nicholas did the same with Yasmine.

'Come on, we need to get you home,' Amelia said.

'What's the rush?' Sophie asked.

'It's just come on the news,' Amelia started, 'people are seeing objects in the sky, ghosts walking round cities, some lunatic said he even saw a wizard turning someone invisible! Honestly, what with all this and the blackout earlier on this week; it's like living here twenty years ago!'

The smiles that had appeared on Yasmine and Clara's faces quickly disappeared. It was beginning and they were nowhere near ready; just the three of them taking on all that? They stood no chance.

'Are you two coming around again tomorrow?' Yasmine asked through slightly gritted teeth, implying that the correct answer was a strong 'yes'.

'Mum, can I?' Sophie pleaded. Her mum nodded.

'Me too dad?' Clara asked.

'Of course you can, you must have missed your friends terribly these last few weeks,' Matthew replied, still a bit confused having had his memories not line up yet, 'I think your dad and I will be taking these implants out for a bit. They seem to have caused us no end of trouble lately!'

The girls all nodded at each other, hinting that they were ready to go. The three hugged again and Sophie and Clara made for the front door with their respective parent.

Sophie got into her dad's car and closed her eyes. What had she done? She thought and thought but couldn't think of anything that she could have done differently. Her friend was safe but now the world was not. She could do something about the world now that she had the implant if she wanted, but if she had lost Katie then there would have been nothing that she could have done and that helped her to relax a bit more.

The car pulled off and Sophie went home, exhausted. It was just getting started though; it looked like it was going to be a busy weekend!

Chapter 30 – Monday Morning

Monday morning came around and Sophie, Yasmine and Clara were sat at the back of Class 6 like it was any normal day. Mrs Tabard was at the front, covering the class again as Miss Sissins had phoned in ill and Mrs Tabard had jumped at the chance to cover the children again. The girls of course knew better than to think that Miss Sissins was ill; they knew she was preparing to save the world.

   They had spent the vast majority of the weekend at Yasmine's house, in her bedroom, plugged into their implants. Every time Yasmine's mum or dad had walked in to check on them, the three of them were zoned out, doing things that 10-year-old girls do. The girls again knew better. They had actually lived the last two days as two months (through the use of the time dilators Miss Sissins had temporarily installed into their implants. She said that using the dilators too much would have an adverse effect on them like Clara's house if they weren't careful) and had been practising the various skills required to make them agents. They had done everything from physical thinking challenges like the minotaur one last week to emotional/empathy training where they could put themselves into someone else's shoes and see things from their point of view – Sophie had found this one particularly interesting. Also, they had started their combat training, so if any bullies were going to try and mess with them they would have no problem dealing with them; however, Miss Sissins had explicitly told them that that was most definitely not what it was for and pointed out that they would need to be projected through the implant, for it to work anyway, unless they really, really mastered it.

Although they had been doing it for two months (in their world) they were still novices and had a lot more training to do. They had also discussed new recruits and getting help to deal with the imminent threats. Miss Sissins had agreed that children would be best as they were a lot more open to things and weren't as obsessed with fame, money and whatever else could inhibit their ability to protect the world but she also wanted to make sure they weren't the sort of children to fail because if they did, she knew King would be back to ruin them. So, they all agreed to keep a look out through their experiences for anyone deemed worthy enough to join team Shadow. However, the girls, and Miss Sissins, had agreed that the agency should no longer just be about stopping threats but also developing human understanding and researching other, better ways of living.

'To prevent is one thing, to understand is another', Sophie had said and that brought her right back to the very start of her adventure. She had wanted more knowledge and wanted to better herself and here she was, giving herself the perfect way to do it.

Over the course of the weekend, various news reports had highlighted some minor problems like Amelia had spoken about that had got people talking about the olden days again. One man had had his shopping stolen by a 'goblin'. An old lady had seen strange lights in the sky and was convinced that there had been an alien pointing at her 'in a threatening manner'. There was nothing huge, the biggest conversation was still about the blackout and how that seemed to have started everything off again. The girls knew though, through Miss Sissins and what she had given them to read about events of the past, that something a lot more ominous must be coming and it would be up to them to stop it. They had a duty; they had chosen to save their friend and so they should be the ones to put it right. Any one of the horrific creatures that they had set free could come back. Miss Sissins guessed that a lot of them would just go home or hide away and not come back through fear of getting caught and locked up in Zatvor again but there were some things in there that would be hell bent on doing terrible things to the Earth before they had been locked in prison, never mind having spent years in there, and for that reason, Miss Sissins knew that they would undoubtedly be back. For now, though, it was quiet.

The hullabaloo around Sophie from just a week ago had died down almost completely, she was never going to go unrecognised but at least, for now, she was no longer front-page news, the world had other things to start worrying about. She had been stopped in the street a couple of times over the weekend, but it hadn't bothered her as it could have been worse. The odd photo with people or the odd question about what she thought happened she could live with. She obviously lied about the answer!

One thing that *was* bothering all three of them, as they sat in the first maths lesson of the week, though was that Katie wasn't at school. They hadn't heard anything from her all weekend. In one of their breaks from using the implant for training, Sophie, Yasmine and Clara had walked round to her house together, to see if she wanted to spend time with them – she hadn't been in and neither had her mum (they checked for perception filters but there wasn't one). They hadn't heard from her since they put her in the car the other night. Miss Sissins had tracked the car and told them that it had got to her house and that her mum had taken her in. However, her mum's implant had turned off not long after and she had lost track of the pair of them. The girls were worried, they missed their friend, and they hadn't treated her like one recently. She had come to them a few times and wanted to tell them something, but the girls had shrugged her off for something they thought was more important. They were all desperate to find her but had no idea where to start.

Reuben Houghton wasn't at school either. No one at school had seen him at all on Friday so the girls thought he must have run home after the upset of what he saw. They had sent him messages asking him if he was alright, but they hadn't heard anything back. Miss Sissins had tracked his implant and said that he was at home and hadn't left since Friday so at least the girls knew where he was.

The last thing Sophie, Yasmine, Clara and Miss Sissins had agreed on was a name change. They no longer wanted to be known as Shadow. It sounded too dark, too much like a dodgy criminal. Miss Sissins had pointed out that she had never liked the name and thought it was in drastic need of a rethink. Having sat round discussing it one afternoon over the last "two months" Sophie had written down all the words she could think of that summed up the new look agency and thought that she might have come up with a new name.

As she looked around the classroom at her two friends, who seemed to be as distracted as she was, a red light flashed in the corner of her eye. Yasmine and Clara had clearly got the same thing as they reacted almost identically as Sophie did and they nearly fell off their chairs. Once they had composed themselves, they looked at each other one more time and smiled the biggest smiles they could – Miss Sissins needed them.

The bell went for dinner time and Mrs Tabard dismissed everyone. The three of them ran onto the field, found a quiet spot and zoned out while lying on the grass.

They arrived in the headquarters at the newly named S.C.O.P.E. (Special Children who Oversee and Protect Earth) to see what this potential first mission could be.

Epilogue 1 - 10 Years Ago - 60 Minutes Before "The Departure"

'I can't get you out immediately,' the woman Desmerelda only knew as Jane said to her calmly, 'but I can look to get it done as soon as possible. I just need you to stay here for a few nights first.'

'In this horrible cess pit of a prison?' Desmerelda replied, not quite believing what she was hearing. 'I haven't done anything wrong have I?' she asked, almost oblivious to what was going on.

She could remember she was putting her baby boy, Kingsley, to bed when a changeling (a mythical that stole children in the night) had blown the side of her house away and tried to take her son. Fortunately, this 'Jane' had shown up and somehow prevented the changeling from spiriting away her only child to the underworld. She couldn't thank her enough but now she was being locked up for what she could see as just looking after her son.

'There's a chance that because we stopped the changeling from spiriting away mid flow that some of her powers might have rubbed off on you – it was a pretty large explosion. We need to get you looked at. There isn't enough room in our medical wards at the moment, but we will keep you safe in here. Everything you're going through should have been dealt with by somebody else. I am not completely familiar with your case.'

Her calm demeanour reassured Desmerelda at her first but, as Jane went on, she became less and less relaxed.

'But what about my boy?' Desmerelda asked.

'He's fine, he's being looked after by the very best. Would you like to see him?' Jane asked.

'My god, yes!' Desmerelda sighed the biggest sigh of relief since her ordeal had started.

Jane put her finger to her ear as she shepherded Desmerelda into what would be her temporary home for the next few nights. 'Send the boy to my PDA... Yes, that boy.'

As Jane moved to the exit and slid the door shut on her cell, she handed Desmerelda a tiny computer screen, no bigger than a mobile phone. On it was a video feed of her son, he was laughing and being looked after by two kind-looking older people.

'Oh, my boy, I'll see you soon,' Desmerelda whispered, kissed her hand and touched the screen.

'Where am I?' Desmerelda asked, feeling more assured that her son was ok.

'We call it Zatvor,' Jane replied, 'There are some dangerous creatures in here. You may have seen some on the news. We will seal you in so that none of them can get to you and we will have you out in no time.'

Mere seconds later, she heard Jane whisper 'She's in, lock it up.'

Desmerelda moved for the door, 'You'll have me out soon, won't you?' she pleaded.

'Of course, we will,' Jane replied, 'we will get you back to your son as soon as possible. If you show any side effects though, you need to let an agent know by pressing the button on that device,' Jane pointed at the PDA she had just given to her.

'What kind of side effects?' Desmerelda assumed Jane was talking about what had happened in the explosion when the changeling had disappeared, however she had no idea what these potential side effects were.

'You'll possibly have visions of the one child you want the most, in your case – Kingsley. This is primitive changeling behaviour – they become fanatical about one child until they have spirited them away into the underworld. The power dampeners here at Zatvor should hopefully limit you to just the visions. We will have you out before anything else more dramatic happens!'

'So, I'll be able to see my son?' she asked excitedly.

'Potentially, but that would mean that you have merged with the changeling in a much more complex way.'

Jane quickly destroyed what Desmerelda was seeing as a blessing, 'Worst of all you might even get the power to spirit people away – but that will definitely be kept calm by the dampeners we have here, which limit all creatures' powers.'

With tears in her eyes, Desmerelda hoped this would be only temporary and so agreed to sit down in the cell and keep herself to herself for the short time she would be here. She had seen some distinctly unappealing characters on the walk through the prison to her cell.

'Thank you,' she said to Jane who simply nodded.

'Remember, press the button if you feel anything unusual,' were Jane's parting words.

Desmerelda turned away from the door and sat down on her bed. The walls were brown, noises reverberated all around her. Squeals, screams and howls adorned the air.

'It's only temporary,' she said to herself.

She tried her best to recall what had happened.

Having heard a noise coming from her son's room she had ventured upstairs to find this demon standing over him. It was hideously deformed; its nose dominated the small part of its face she saw. The rest was hidden by long, greasy brown hair and the hood on its cloak. The hands that emerged from under the cloak had only three stumpy fingers each and were smothered in warts. She then remembered the cackle that emanated from its mouth as it began to spirit away her son to the underworld. It sent a shiver down her spine and she cried for the first time since it had happened.

She dried her eyes and, for a brief, split second, Kingsley lay there on the bed next her. Knowing this was her first vision, Desmerelda picked up the button and pressed it. The changeling powers were beginning...

Epilogue 2 – Where Katie Went

When Katie had arrived back at her house, her mum, Tasha, wasn't worried. Over the summer, Katie had played out with Sophie and Jasmine a lot and had come home at about this time every night.

Tasha didn't notice Katie get out of the car and only realised she was home when she came into the kitchen and sat down at the table. Tasha carried on washing the dishes.

'Good day?' Tasha asked.

Katie shrugged. She was tired despite having just woken up from something.

'Have you heard from Dad?' Katie asked, completely out of the blue.

Tasha put the last of the dishes on the side and sat at the table opposite her. Katie never asked about her dad. Tasha had always said that she would tell her everything she knew and she had. There had been nothing new happen since they last saw each other that morning.

'No,' Tasha replied, gently, 'You know I'd tell you if I had.'

Tasha put her hand on Katie's and tried to work out what was wrong with her daughter.

However, before she could ask any more, a bright blue light appeared to wrap itself around Katie and in the blink of an eye she disappeared from Tasha's view. Panic set in for Tasha.

Before she knew it, the blue light appeared again albeit this time around herself. It encased her from head to toe and contained small blue balls of energy racing around in circles all around her. Tasha ran her fingers over it and tried to step out from it but couldn't. A few seconds later, the light had disappeared and Tasha found herself and Katie in an enormous room that appeared to be the bridge of a ship. There was a huge screen at the front, lots of monitors round the edge of the room and four black chairs in the centre. In the middle of the four black chairs was a much bigger one – clearly the one for the person in charge.

Before Tasha could say anything, from over by one of the monitors round the edge, a woman started to move towards them. She was dressed all in black and had bright white hair and red eyes. She was slender and almost glided across the room.

Looking Tasha straight in the eye, the lady could tell that she and Katie were frightened and so spoke gently.

'You must be Sophie,' the lady said to Tasha, offering a soft smile of sympathy.

'Me?' Tasha stuttered, 'No, my name is Tasha... Tasha Green.'

The lady looked somewhat confused and tilted her head for a second before her eyes started to light up and a realisation seemingly dawned on her.

With a huge smile, she turned to Katie, 'Then *you*, my sweet, must be Sophie?'

Katie mumbled something incomprehensible even to herself as nerves crept over her.

'It's ok,' the lady said, 'I understand you must be scared but it's ok, honestly...'

The lady kept talking but Katie wasn't listening. There was far too much to take in. The next thing that Katie realised was that her mum had stepped in front of her to almost act like a human shield.

'Do not block my way,' the woman said, 'I am addressing the young lady. I mean her no harm.'

Tasha did her best to look scary and intimidating but the lady just looked straight through her and walked closer to Katie.

The lady started to mutter something to herself, incomprehensible to Tasha and Katie.

'She said she…' Tasha appealed.

'I SAID STOP!' the lady shouted at Tasha, who fell backwards slightly, 'ALLOW THE CHILD TO SPEAK FOR HERSELF! I AM HERE TO HELP HER!'

It was then that Katie could see that she and her mum might be in danger and found the courage to speak, 'I'm not Sophie but I do know her and where you can find her. My name is Katie… Miss,' she said as confidently as she could, but also sensing that she should be talking to the lady with respect.

Katie then switched off from her surroundings again as a bolt of adrenaline rocketed through her and then out again and so the lady's words were lost to her.

Quickly getting her head back together as her emotions ran wild, Katie tuned back in to what the lady was saying.

'Welcome aboard Katie,' the lady said with open arms, 'my name is… Condenar.'

Printed in Great Britain
by Amazon